THE LADIES OF BATH

The Duke's Daughter ~ Lady Amelia Atherton

The Baron in Bath ~ Miss Julia Bellevue

The Deceptive Earl ~ Lady Charity Abernathy

THE HAWTHORNE SISTERS

The Forbidden Valentine ~ Lady Eleanor

THE BAGGINGTON SISTERS

The Countess and the Baron ~ Prudence

Almost Promised ~ Temperance

The Healing Heart ~ Mercy

The Lady to Match a Rogue ~ Faith

NETTLEFOLD CHRONICLES

Not Quite a Lady; Not Quite a Knight

Stitched in Love

OTHER NOVELS BY ISABELLA THORNE

The Mad Heiress and the Duke ~ Miss Georgette Quinby

The Duke's Wicked Wager ~ Lady Evelyn Evering

CONTENTS

THE MAD HEIRESS AND THE DUKE

The
Mad Heiress
and the
Duke

Miss Georgette Quinby

Isabella Thorne

A Regency Romance Novel

The Mad Heiress and the Duke ~ Miss Georgette Quinby
A Regency Romance Novel

All rights reserved.

2016 Mikita Associates Publishing

Published in the United States of America.

www.isabellathorne.com

Part 1

Meeting the Duke

*G*eorgette had escaped to the garden. Even in winter, the green and growing things gave her comfort. She breathed slowly through her nose. Her breath puffed out like a little cloud. No doubt the tongues would be wagging. The *Ton* would think her even crazier than normal to come out here in the cold, but she needed a moment, just a moment to herself. In the cold winter air she could have some time to gather her wits about her, to take some deep breaths. To remember who she was and how it had once been; how she had once been so blindingly happy, and then to remember how it was now.

Breathe, she told herself as she pressed her gloved hands together over her stomacher. In. Out. Well, in as far as her corset allowed and then out.

The ballroom had been stifling. An absolute crush, packed with bodies and warring perfumes. And all of them turning their catty faces to her, looking at her with disdain. She could not bear it for one moment longer.

"Look, it's the Mad Heiress," one of the young ladies had said tittering like a ninny.

"Is it really? I thought she'd killed herself." Her friend fanned herself as she looked slyly over the accessory at Georgette.

"No, you were misinformed," another said, craning her bejeweled neck. "I heard she flung herself off a parapet, after Lord Falks threw her over for Lady Judith."

"I heard it was a cliff," the first one said.

"I'm certain it was a parapet. But no matter. The point is, she survived."

"Poor thing. I'd rather be dead," said the first woman fanning herself quite vigorously.

"It was a flight of stairs," Georgette had said to the open air, once she had fled to the garden. "Stairs. If one must gossip, at the very least one should get the facts straight. I flung myself down a stairway."

She should probably stop talking to herself, she thought. She was already known as The Mad Heiress, and she hadn't done anything exciting for almost ten years. Lud, if the *Ton* heard her grumbling to herself about stairs she would never rest in peace.

But honestly, a cliff? If it had been a cliff, she might have had some success. Instead, she had woken up in her bed, several days later, with a sore head and a broken hip, like an old woman. And a fiancé who did not love her. She must not forget that.

Oh, Sebastien. Why?

Ten years ago she had been slipping out of ballrooms

to meet him in the garden, the stolen kisses sweet on her lips. Escaping the candlelight and the weak punch and her stifling mother, hoping for a stolen moment with her beloved.

Ten years, and no one forgot. No one ever forgot. She clenched her fists. She would forever be The Mad Heiress. No matter that she had been barely seventeen when Sebastien had informed her that his heart belonged to another. No matter that she was twenty-six-years old now, and a chaperone, a spinster, firmly on the shelf. No matter that she could not conceive of the sensibility and passion that had driven her up those stairs. She could not remember, but everyone else still remembered.

Deep breaths, she reminded herself as she rubbed her gloved hands over her cooling arms. Breathe in, breathe out. Or, rather, breathe in as deeply as one's corset allows, and breathe out. In, and out, through the nose.

Georgette froze. She sniffed the air. Someone was smoking a cigar.

Oh, bother.

She swallowed. Perhaps the gentleman would not realize she'd entered the gardens. She could surreptitiously sneak back into the ballroom. She made to turn back into the house.

He stood right in front of her. Grey flecked through his hair. She knew his eyes were dark blue, but the darkness of the garden made them almost black. He peered at her with them, over a royal, aquiline nose.

The Duke of Eversley.

"I beg your pardon," he said. "I did not realize there was a lady in the garden. I will snuff my cigar."

"Please do not trouble yourself on my account, Your Grace," she said, giving a curtsy. "I was just about to re-enter the ballroom."

He blinked at her. "I know you," he said. He tilted his head and looked at her, no doubt attempting to place her face.

Georgette opened her mouth and then closed it again. Did he truly not recognize her?

"Ah, yes, Your Grace," she said. "I do believe we crossed paths several years ago, when I was newly out."

He continued to look at her curiously.

"I was engaged to your dear friend, Lord Sebastien Falks."

"Sebastien? But you cannot have been engaged to Sebastien, he married my sister..."

Georgette knew the moment he pieced it together, the moment he remembered. The Duke colored, though it was difficult to tell in the darkness, and gave a small cough.

"I do beg your pardon," he said. "I forgot, you see. It was all so long ago."

She couldn't help herself: she laughed. He stared at her for a moment as if she were demented.

"I am so sorry," she said. "I do not mean to laugh at you. It is only that I was just musing at how much time has passed and yet no one has forgotten. It is on the tips of all the gossips' tongues. And then you appeared and you did not remember."

She laughed once more. "It's so terribly refreshing," she said, "to learn that at least one person might forget."

She gave a final curtsy. "I do beg your pardon, Your Grace," she said. "Please finish your cigar. I am happy to have seen you again, after all this time."

CHARLES POMFREY, The Sixth Duke of Eversley, watched the dark-haired lady return to the ball as he puffed on his cigar.

Ten years. It must have been almost ten years since he saw her last. Right before Blanche left for Paris. Yes. He remembered now.

"*La petite Mademoiselle*," Blanche had called her. "Sebastien," she had said to his dear friend, "you must know I adore your betrothed." She clasped her hands together with glee. "*Tres jolie*. And so passionate. Why, she positively hops every time she sees you, Sebastien. As if she cannot contain herself."

"She has a good deal of money, Blanche," Sebastien had said in reply. "She can afford to hop."

The Duke shook his head. Poor Sebastien. So handsome, so charming, so desperately in need of funds. So much so, that he threw over his young heiress fiancé to run off with a duke's sister blessed with an even greater dowry.

Still, Sebastien and his sister Judith appeared to suit each other well enough. Judith provided the funds and the beauty and the ducal connection, while Sebastien provided...well, to be honest, he was not certain as to what Sebastien provided, but Judith had never complained. Indeed, he did believe his sister loved the man.

Their elopement had been quite the scandal nearly a decade ago. He knew this. And yet, he did not remember it. That time was forever shrouded for him; a dark, foggy period to which he did not dare return.

He shook himself and gave his arms a slap. Mustn't dwell on the past. The garden was cold, and his cigar was almost out.

Where was White? Meeting the man was the whole reason he was here, standing in the garden. When he had returned to England, he'd hoped to retreat to one of his estates, to lick his wounds. Instead, he had been asked to meet in the garden, outside a ball.

"Eversley." A man stepped out from the shadows. The Duke wondered how long he had been there. With Mr. White, one never really knew; the man was a ghost.

The Duke nodded.

"It's good to see you walking once again," White said. "I will not lie: for some time there, I thought we had lost you."

"Fortunate for me that a doctor in Vienna did not share your belief," Eversley said.

"Indeed, indeed." Mr. White rubbed his hands together.

The Duke peered in through the wavy glass pane, to the well-lit ballroom. Inside, people danced the minuet, and country dances. They joined hands and smiled and laughed. They flirted and teased. He had once been one of them.

"I'll be brief," Mr. White said. "It appears that a list was at one point prepared."

"A list," The Duke said.

"Containing certain, ahh...names." White removed a monocle from his pocket. He breathed on the glass to fog it up, and then removed a handkerchief. Methodically, he began wiping it down, every once in a while stopping to breathe on it once more.

The Duke could see his own breath in the cold night air, lit by the moon. How many times had he stood outside ballrooms and assemblies, theatres and cafes and coffee shops, in the dark, to have brief and secret conversations, lit only by moonlight or faint torches, spare lanterns, small candles? He'd lost count. He'd begun to feel that he would forever conduct his life in cold darkness.

"Your name is on this list," White said.

The Duke looked up. "This list...what exactly is its nature?"

"I think you might hazard a guess." White tucked the monocle back in his waistcoat. "I should correct myself. All of your names were on the list."

A list of all of his names. And the others. No. It could not be.

Some fool had written down a list of spies for the Kingdom.

"Who on earth would be so daft as to write down all the names?" The Duke exploded.

Mr. White stared at the Duke in silence.

"We are not to question His Highness's reasoning," he finally said.

The Duke swore softly. "What is being done?"

"The fortunate news is that it appears that the individual who took the list is more of a mercenary bent than a patriotic one. Our intelligence has led us to believe that a man, who goes by the name of Lightfoot, is arranging to sell the list to the French."

"And we aim to stop him."

"Precisely. We believe that Lightfoot is a Mr. Meryton. However, of that we do not have conclusive proof. There are one or two other suspects."

"Merry? Merry Meryton, a spy for France? Inconceivable." The Duke stabbed out his cigar. Eversley had known Merry for years, and thought he knew him well. They had been once friends.

"It appears Mr. Meryton has been gambling considerably recently. I imagine he has amassed considerable debts and must be quite desperate to pay them," Mr. White said. "We believe that, if he does have the list, he will be trying to obtain the highest price possible as soon as he can. The transfer is likely to happen very soon."

"What do you wish for me to do?" The Duke asked.

"You are in the fortunate position of being able to navigate all levels of society," Mr. White said. "We do not know how and when Mr. Meryton will try to sell the letter, or to whom he will be selling. We merely ask that you track him and prevent him from doing so."

"Oh? Is that all?"

Mr. White sniffed. "I will be in touch if I learn anything else. In the meantime, I suppose you should return to the ball. You could ask the lady you were speaking with a moment ago to dance. Then again, perhaps not. Did she not toss herself off a bridge over your brother-in-law?"

"Stairs," the Duke said, remembering how she had grumbled to herself before realizing his presence in the garden. "She tossed herself down a staircase."

_____

2

*T*hank heavens for potted plants, Georgette thought. She was seated next to just such a thing, no doubt normally kept in a greenhouse. She was enjoying her relative seclusion. From her current vantage point, she could only see half of the ballroom sneaking glances at her while pretending not to see her at all, as opposed to the entire room.

She had forgotten how it felt to be the subject of such gossip. After her tumble almost a decade ago, she had been the subject of much staring and gossip. Slowly, however, the people in the village of Highfield had begun to turn their attentions to other matters. They no longer looked askance at her, or discussed her foolish behavior. Occasionally a new visitor to the county would ask her to dance, or express interest, and the gossip would be renewed, but generally it had become manageable.

This was likely why Fanny had believed they would

survive the gossip of Town. Georgette did try to tell her cousin that she would not make the best chaperone.

"I'm afraid my presence will affect your own reputation," she had told her younger cousin.

"Oh bother," Fanny had said. "I don't mind a spot of scandal, and I'd much rather you than Aunt Agatha."

Georgette had grimaced and relented. An actual dragon would be better than Aunt Agatha. Fanny, who had suffered under the attentions of their terrible aunt the previous year when she made her debut, was desperate for an alternative and so Georgette capitulated.

Still, she imagined that neither she nor Fanny had fully appreciated how much the *Ton* loved to remember terrible behavior. She was a pariah. The only thing coming close to her was the potted plant.

She peered into the plant. It was the standard ballroom greenery. Someone had tucked a small, folded-up paper note in amongst the leaves. It must be a love note, she mused. Much like the ones Sebastien used to pass her at just such events. Only he would usually pass them to her as he bent over her hand for a kiss. She smiled remembering.

Sneakily, she reached in between the leaves and drew the paper out. For a moment, she experienced a momentary pang of guilt. This was someone else's note. She should not be intruding.

Oh, bother. All she wanted to do was read it. That wasn't so very bad, was it? Under the cover of her fan, she opened it.

20-6-1-21-21-12 8-21-6-18-1,
21-6-5-6-20-20-6-10. 18-6-6-18.

Oh how delightful! A cryptogram. She wished she could work on it right now. She could not, however, not with the ball taking place around her. But surely she could copy the numbers down, to play with later? Carefully, she picked up her programme. No gentleman had dared scrawl his name upon it, and so there was plenty of space for her to quickly jot down the numbers with her pencil. Once done, she surreptitiously folded the note back up and snuck it back into the plant.

There. No one had seen that, had they? She looked around the ballroom, attempting to appear casual. No. No one showed any signs of having seen her. In fact, most of the heads were craning towards one side of the room, near the garden doors.

A pair of heads moved slightly, and then she could see what drew all of the attention: the Duke of Eversley had stepped into the room.

"Heavens, if he isn't just the handsomest gentlemen you've seen, girls," a matron to the left of Georgette said to her daughters.

"And so very well endowed," a woman on the other side of the potted plant said to her tittering friends.

"I assume you mean his estates," her friend responded.

"Why, certainly, whatever else could I have meant?" the woman asked, with a wink.

And he was. Georgette had forgotten how striking he appeared. Every inch the Duke.

"But mama," one of the daughters said, "I thought he was in mourning."

The matron nodded. "He was, Dearie. For nigh on ten years. What a tragedy, his young wife dying. We saw neither hide nor hair of him since. But now the word is that he is recovered, and in desperate need of a wife."

"He appears to be coming this way," one of the other daughters said.

"Oh, so he is! Stand up straight, girls. Look angelic."

One of the daughters let out a muffled snort, but they did as they were told.

Georgette watched them, hiding her own grin. They were so young and fresh, so terribly eager. She could remember giggling with her cousin Anne in a similar manner, and being chastised by her own mother.

So distracted was she by her musings, that she did not realize where the Duke was headed. Not until he stopped right in front of her. He gave a small bow.

Georgette's mouth popped open. Her cheeks bloomed with dismay. Swiftly she got to her feet and curtsied.

"I apologize, Your Grace," she said. "I was distracted and did not realize you were standing in front of me."

The corners of his mouth twitched.

"Please," he said, "do not concern yourself." He leaned forward conspiratorially. "I thought that, rather than force people to choose which one of us they want to ogle, we might join forces and allow them to gape at us together."

Georgette blinked and then grinned. "So terribly kind of you to consider the guests," she said.

"I would ask you to dance," he said. "But I am afraid I

was injured last year, and am not able to move especially gracefully."

She waved her hand airily. "I would have had to refuse," she said, "as my hip troubles me when I dance."

"Perhaps we might sit this one out, then?"

"That sounds lovely," she said.

⟶◦⟨⟨⟩⟩◦⟵

EVERSLEY GESTURED at Georgette to sit and she did. He followed suit, flourishing his coat-tails out, before settling down upon the chair corner.

He had forgotten how pretty she looked. In the dark of the garden he had not been able to see all of her, although he had recognized her form and her manner of holding herself. Her hair and eyes were still brown, and she still had a dimple on her right cheek. Still, many of the elements had changed somewhat over time, he realized, which may have been why he initially had some difficulty placing her. She was softer around the edges now. Less coltish, less eager. Fewer calf's eyes, less in love.

"I must extend my sympathies, Your Grace," she said. "I overheard a conversation just now alluding to your deceased wife. I was unaware Her Grace had passed."

He gave a wry smile. "I imagine that the reason I had trouble remembering your connection to my sister and friend is the same reason you were unaware of my own tragedy. I believe they happened close together in time."

Her eyes widened. "So long ago?" she asked.

He shrugged.

She shook her head. "I apologize," she said. "I did not intend to pry."

"Blanche returned to France in August of 1793," he said.

"Oh," she said understanding instantly. "Oh, no. I didn't realize...I am so sorry."

"She was killed," he said. "She did not pass away." He hated when people said that Blanche passed away. As if she had simply drifted off in her sleep. But she hadn't. She had lost her head.

Miss Quinby placed a gloved hand over his, no doubt without even realizing it. He looked down at it, wondering what her hand was doing there, why it should feel comforting.

Stop it. Think of something else.

"And you?" he asked, deciding to turn the tables. "You flung yourself off...a balcony, was it?"

"Stairs," she said, through gritted teeth. "I flung myself down a flight of stairs."

He grinned. "I know," he said. "I heard you in the garden."

For a second her face froze and he wondered if she would slap him. He should not have made jest of her despair. And despair it must have been, for her to have done such a thing. But then she smiled. It seemed irrepressible, her smile.

"I should cut you direct," she said, "for laughing at my ill-fated attempt to end my life. It was quite tragic, if you must know. I was unconscious for days."

His hand tightened on hers.

"Now you have made me feel quite the heel," he said.

"Good," she said. "Since I have done so, I will share something with you I have not told another soul. I am telling you this because I quite liked Her Grace."

She took a deep breath and spoke quickly. "I did not mean to fling myself down the stair"

He blinked. "Er...," he began.

"Oh, I did mean to end my life," she said. "I had intended to toss myself off the roof, you see. I was extremely distraught and having a fit, and I declared that I could not live another day without Sebastien. I did not feel I could bear it. I was running up to the roof when I tripped and tumbled down the stair."

"You tripped."

"I did." She nodded. "By the time I recovered the damage was done, the gossip was out. But I learned an important lesson, while I was asleep."

"Oh? And what would that be?" he asked.

"I truly believed I could not survive another day without Sebastien's love. But, the fall showed me that I could. Granted, those were days when I was unaware of the world around me, but they were days nonetheless. I had survived, without him. Furthermore, I realized that I had been surviving without his love for quite some time. I simply had not known."

"And so you decided to remain among the living," he said.

"Indeed. I decided that I would continue to live, to the very best of my ability. With one tiny resolution."

He waited.

"I resolved to never again fall in love," she said. "My heart and my vanity, if we are being entirely honest, could not withstand another such tragedy. Never again will I sacrifice my pride for another."

"Why then, my dear Miss Quinby, the two of us have something in common. I myself made a similar resolution after losing my wife. Never again shall I fall in love."

Out of the corner of his eye, he could see Mr. Merry Meryton, slipping from the room. He had to follow.

Eversley stood, still holding her hand. Bowing, he brought it to his lips. "I hope to see you again soon, Miss Quinby" he said.

"Yes," she said. "Likewise, Your Grace"

The Duke exited the ball in time to hear Meryton's directions to his driver. He then hopped into his own carriage.

"St. James's place," he said to Mr. Murphy. "We're to follow Meryton."

"Very good, Your Grace," Mr. Murphy said.

Mr. Murphy had been with the Duke for almost twenty years, and had followed him to France. It had been Murphy who dragged him, drunk out of his mind, out of clubs and halls in the days following Blanche's death. It had been Murphy who posted lookout in France as the Duke scaled walls and fences. And it had been Murphy who had picked up the Duke, unconscious and bleeding profusely from the wound in his side, and driven him to safety.

Merry Meryton was not especially difficult to follow. After entering Moneykin's, a gentleman's gambling club, he posted up at a whist table, and did not leave for several hours.

Eversley, who only gambled when it was necessary, took a glass of wine and prowled the edges of the room. Men nodded to him and bowed. Some stopped to speak, but most kept their distance. He had not been in London for such a long time; no doubt his reappearance after his prolonged absence was unsettling for some.

Every once in a while, to keep any questioning eyes at bay, he would play a round of faro. It was during one such round that he saw an old friend from Eton, Lord Simon Brockton.

"I say, old boy," Lord Brockton said to Eversley as he gave him a hearty pat on the back. "Good to have you in town. We'll be looking forward to seeing you at Lords."

Eversley blinked. "Right," he said. Lords. He had duties in Parliament. Neglected duties, if he was honest about it.

When Blanche had died, he had been so intent upon exacting revenge on those who had betrayed her that he had ignored his many duties back home in England. To be sure, nothing was ruined. There were no estates lying in disrepair, no tenants starving. He had very capable stewards and secretaries tending to his estates and business. But he had been sadly uninvolved. When he had been injured in France and brought home after his convalescence in Austria, he had realized just how lost he felt. What was he to do? He prowled his rooms as if he would see Blanche appear, but she was sadly lost, and so was he.

And then he had received the note from Mr. White, requesting his assistance, and he had felt relief. This was something he knew how to do: espionage. But it was one thing to do it in France, undercover. It was another to roam a gambling hall in London as a duke. Everyone was bowing at him; men were speaking of horse races and boxing matches they assumed he knew about; and Simon Brockton was asking when he would be appearing in chambers.

He nodded to Brockton and returned to his cards. The dealer was cheating; he was sure of it, but he was not inclined to draw attention to it. He had learned how to avoid attention, over the years.

Not that he had avoided it tonight. He grinned into his cards. He had known exactly what he was doing when he had walked over to Miss Quinby. She had looked so solitary, so alone. He remembered when she was young and first out. She had always been surrounded by people, cousins and friends. By Sebastien and his ilk. He could still picture her, laughing gaily as Sebastien kissed the inside of her wrist, Judith looking on unhappily.

Blanche had known. "Careful, Sebastian," she had said. "You play with that one's heart."

"I don't wish to play with her heart," Sebastian had said. "I wish to play with her pocketbook."

He should have seen; he should have put a stop to it. It was so simple in retrospect. He should have granted his sister more freedom. Instead, he had told Judith that he would not be allowing any offers of marriage until she was eighteen. Sebastian, desperate for money, had landed Miss Quinby. But Judith, determined to not let him marry another, persuaded Sebastian that her brother would relent once they were married.

And he had. Overwhelmed with worry for his wife in

France, Eversley had not spared a thought to the note he received regarding their elopement to Gretna. His secretary had stood nervously in his office, wondering what he would like to do; whether he would allow his friend to ruin his sister.

"Settle the debts," Eversley had said. "Put them on an allowance." And then he had left for France, pretending to be a commoner, hoping to smuggle his wife and her family back to England. But Blanche was already dead.

Meryton was within his sights, still playing whist. The man hadn't even stood up to use the chamber pot. At this rate, it was going to be a very long night.

erry Meryton visited two more halls before the night was out. Daylight was breaking by the time Meryton returned to his bachelor's digs in the Albany apartments and the Duke was able to walk the short distance to his mansion in Mayfair.

"Ah, James," the Duke said to his footman, as he entered his London home. He could hear the sounds of a house just awakening, clatter in the kitchens, the chambermaids scrubbing out fires. "If you could be so good as to stand guard outside the Albany, I am going to attempt some sleep."

"Yes, Your Grace," James said.

Once given a description of Meryton and orders to alert Eversley and Murphy the moment there was sign of activity, James departed.

The Duke made his way up to his chambers. Dawn light was just breaking through the windows, hitting the high bed and the elaborate furniture which decorated the room. He waved off his valet's offer to help him undress, and stood alone, looking about, thinking of his dead wife.

"There you are," he said at last.

Blanche was lying on a settee near the fire. One of her hands hung limply at her side, still holding a novel. The other rested on her stomacher. She had dozed off reading her novel, waiting for him.

He stared at her, so lovely in the early morning light. Her blonde hair was loose, a cascade of ringlets along the back of the settee. Her lips were softly parted, until they closed as she suddenly woke up. She smiled, stretched, and rubbed her eyes, letting the book fall to the floor, where it disappeared into the air.

"You were gone all night," she said. "I waited."

He grunted. He itched to reach out to her, but he knew he couldn't touch her. Instead he let his hands run along the edge of the brocaded chair that stood in front of him.

She sat up and looked at him. She cocked her head. "You met someone," she said.

"Yes, Mr. White had yet another task for me. Don't know how he does it. The man is always exactly where he needs to be. Do you remember that time in Marseilles? How on earth did he find me on a roof?"

She smiled. "You know very well that wasn't what I meant, *mon Chér.*"

He strode over and stirred the fire. "I saw Sebastian's former betrothed. She's aged."

"So have you." She sat back against the settee. She stared at him, lightly biting her thumbnail, and yet still managed to flirtatiously grin at him. It was a pose he had seen a thousand times; assessing, cool, and yet there was the tiniest bit of doubt as she worried her thumbnail.

"She tried to kill herself when he threw her over for Judith," he said. "Or, rather, she thought she wanted to, but she tripped during the execution of it."

"She was so passionate," Blanche said. "Always so very full of life, *non*?"

"She was young."

"So were we, once."

"No longer," he said.

She laughed. "You, perhaps. But not me. I will forever be *une jeune fille*."

"You were not," he retorted. "You were married, to a duke, I might remind you. You were a Madame."

She waved her hands. "We were children. *Les enfants*. Playing at Duke and Duchess."

"It was real," he said. "It wasn't play."

Her thumb was back, teasing her lip. "No," she said. "It was real."

He wanted to move to her, to take her hand, to slip it up to his mouth, to kiss her knuckles. To touch her and tell her how much he loved her.

"Blanche," he said. "Oh, Blanche."

How can I live without you?

She smiled; her eyes sad. She shrugged, ever the Frenchwoman.

Because you must.

"Go to sleep, Charles," she said. "You must rest."

And then he watched her, disappear into the morning light, no novel left on the floor, no imprint left in the settee, no lingering scent of her upon the air.

Gone, always and forever. Gone.

He drew a deep, shaky breath. He had to sleep if he wanted to be alert as he trailed Meryton. He stripped off his clothes and fell into bed, pulling the curtains closed, blocking out the world.

There he dreamed of Blanche, laughing and smiling and leaning forward to whisper a secret in the ear of a brunette with a dimple, her eyes alight at the shared confidence.

GEORGETTE STARED at the numbers she had scrawled on her programme.

20-6-1-21-21-12 8-21-6-18-1,
21-6-5-6-20-20-6-10. 18-6-6-18.

A thrill of anticipation swept through her. After she had recovered from tumbling down the stairs at the age of seventeen, she had decided to devote herself to only reasonable pursuits. Mathematics, Latin, and the sciences were allowed. Poetry and painting and novels forbidden. Music she also allowed, because she could not quite bring herself to give it up. But really, when one considered it, music was positively mathematical. More logic than passion, to be sure. And yes, over time she dabbled in a spot of poetry and read a horrid novel or two, but that was long after she was quite recovered and not nearly so overwhelmed by her former sensibility. She could not help it: sometimes Herodotus was just too much of a bore.

Somewhat to her surprise, over the years she had developed a true love of mathematics and logic. Puzzles, number games, tricky problems, she loved them all. Fortunately, the curate of her parish shared her passion, and they had developed a habit of exchanging cryptograms and timing one another.

She looked at the last word. *18-6-6-18*. Novice mistake, she thought. There were few four letter words that began and ended with the same letter, and shared the middle two letters as well. She suspected it was not "peep" or "elle".

The most likely possibility was *N-O-O-N*. This meant that the penultimate word was *21-O-5-O-20-20-O-10*. Considering that "noon," the last word, was a time, there was a strong chance that this word would indicate the day.

T-O-M-O-R-R-O-W.

On her cipher, she filled in the corresponding numbers to match the letters she had used, looking for a pattern.

R-O-8-1-T-T-12 8-T-O- N-1

She chewed on her fingernail as she looked at the first two words. No doubt this indicated a rendezvous, and so this should be the name of a place. But what place?

She looked at the last letter. Not many letters could follow *N*. She had already used *T. Y*, perhaps. Or *E*. Yes, most likely *E*.

R-O-8-E-T-T-12 8-T-O- N-E

There, she thought. Whoever made this cipher

should not have made S correspond with 8. They looked so similar, it was child's play.

ROSETTA STONE,
TOMORROW. NOON.

Almost sadly simple. She sighed. Well, she had finished that.

"What is that you're busy with, Georgette?" Fanny looked over at her. "Did the curate send you another note?"

Georgette smiled. "Something to that effect," she said.

"Heavens, the two of you are dedicated," Fanny said. "You should send him one in return and tell him he may have a competitor for your affections."

"Whatever are you on about?" Georgette asked.

"Why, the Duke, my dear," Fanny said. "It was all anyone could speak of at the ball. He strode right over to you, no by your leave to anyone else in the room, and then sat and spoke with you. And then he kissed your hand. I declare, the entire ballroom buzzed. Positively buzzed, I say. Everyone is so deliciously intrigued. Our dinner invitations have tripled overnight, you must know."

Georgette grinned. "I had no idea," she said. "I fear that everyone will be terribly disappointed to learn the truth of the matter. It was nothing so exciting. He and I were often in each other's company when I was first out. He merely came to speak to me, to commiserate in our mutual tendency to attract gossip."

Fanny gave her a look. "Oh, Do not go telling the

others that," she said. "I am quite enjoying our sudden popularity."

"Very well," Georgette said, agreeably. Fanny could demand it, after standing by Georgette's side over the years. To be sure, Fanny was only eight when everything went so horribly awry, but she had been a very steadfast eight-year-old.

Georgette looked down at the cryptogram again. She had read about the Rosetta Stone. If she wasn't mistaken, it was on display. She chewed her lip.

"Fanny," she said, "what say you to an excursion to the British Museum today?"

"I say it sounds terribly dull, but for you, my dearest cousin, I shall do it," Fanny said. "Only if we might get an ice after."

"But it is winter!"

"I do not give a fig. We are heiresses, Georgette. We may eat ices whenever we so choose."

4

$\mathcal{I}$t was fortunate that Merry Meryton was not an especially early riser. Due to Eversley's dream-plagued sleep, he had been slow to awaken later in the morning.

He shaved and dressed for the day and made his way to Piccadilly to relieve James from his loitering. He had just sent his footman home when Meryton emerged from the Albany and began to walk west with purpose.

At a distance, Eversley followed the man as he made his way through the crowded London streets towards...Bloomsbury? What could the man possibly be looking to do over there?

Ah, he thought, as he watched Merry make his way up the steps into Montague House. It appeared his erstwhile traitor-to-the-crown had an appointment at the British Museum.

The Duke strode up the steps after the man.

"I say, if it isn't Eversley!"

The voice checked him. He stopped and looked at the man speaking.

"Lord Fletcher," Eversley said tightly.

The other man gave a slight bow and the Duke nodded.

"Haven't seen you in London in years, old boy," Fletcher said.

"Ah, no. I have tended to stay in the country." Eversley wondered how soon he could break free. Meryton could be handing over the list this very moment, for all he knew. He watched the crowds surging in and out of the museum.

"You must come and dine with us some evening," Lord Fletcher was saying. Eversley had always found Fletcher to be a bit of a wet blanket. Why would he want to dine at his home? He never had in the past.

"Yes, certainly," he said.

"And we'll see you at the ball, no doubt?"

What ball?

"Lady Fletcher is in quite a state, I must tell you, worrying about the details of it all. But you mustn't repeat that. She would have my hide if she knew I was telling a Duke of all people that she was worried about her hostessing skills."

If only Lady Fletcher knew just how much Eversley was concerned with her hostessing skills, which was not at all, then she might have minded less. He eased back from Fletcher.

"I won't tell a soul," he said. "But I must beg your pardon Fletcher, I was hoping to ah..." He trailed off. Miss Quinby was standing on the steps, looking about.

He turned to Fletcher and bowed. "I will be sure to attend the ball," he said.

Fletcher tapped his nose. "I see you've a lady to attend to," he said. "I shan't keep you."

Eversley bounded up the steps. He took Miss Quinby's hand and raised it to his lips.

"Miss Quinby," he said. "I shall be forever in your debt if you will indulge me and pretend you came here to meet me and are now willing to walk about the museum with me."

She blinked at him, as he bowed over her hand; then smiled. "I suppose I might assist with that," she said. "You may help me locate my cousin. I fear I lost her in the crowd."

He tucked her hand into his elbow and they entered the museum together.

"You see, I dragged Fanny here," she said. "I read a note at the dance, and I was determined to see the trysting lovers, but I did not have any such luck. And then I became so distracted by the conversation of the men behind me, and Fanny said something about a Captain Cook and I waved her off, and now I cannot find her."

He nodded. "Most of what you just said to me I do not understand at all, but you can explain it later. Do you know Merry Meryton, by any chance?"

"Everyone knows Mr. Meryton," she said.

"Have you seen him here?"

"Yes, I believe he came here to see Miss Ditherfield, out from under the nose of her terrifying mother. She is being accompanied today by Miss Palmer, who is a much more manageable chaperone, I must say."

"Are they still here?" Encountering Miss Quinby was getting better and better. She'd provided an excuse to escape Fletcher, was willing to wander around the museum with him, and had seen Meryton.

"I believe so. I imagine they will be here for some time. Stolen moments are to be treasured, are they not?"

He twisted his lips. "I suppose they are," he said.

"Speaking of stolen moments, I overheard a most extraordinary conversation just before you arrived," Miss Quinby said. "I was standing by the Rosetta Stone."

Miss Ditherfield was known to be an heiress. Eversley did not know her well, but nothing he had heard suggested that she or own of her family would be a French spy. Why was Meryton with her? Was he courting her? Did he hope to get his hands on her inheritance? Was he willing to turn traitor to his country for her?

Miss Quinby was still talking. Eversley nodded appreciatively, while he wondered if perhaps Ditherfield was really Delacroix or some other French name. He could ask around.

"And then the one gentleman," Miss Quinby continued. "He said that if he did not see the funds within a fortnight, he would sell the list to someone else."

What?

Eversley stopped walking, his thoughts coming to an abrupt halt.

"I beg your pardon, Miss Quinby. I was woolgathering. I believe I must have missed a portion of what you were relating. Might you repeat it?"

She smiled. "I suspected as much. You kept nodding and saying oh, mmm."

He grinned. "Blanche once threw a boot at me for doing that."

"Did she hit you?"

"She did." He leaned down and showed her a small scar above his eyebrow. "Then she was quite sorry."

She touched the scar with her gloved finger, lightly running over the ridge. "It was your own fault," she said. "If you had been paying attention, she would have felt no need to toss a boot."

"Indeed. But you were saying something about a gentleman and a list."

"Yes, I was. It was on account of the note that I found last night at the ball, you see," she said.

"A note."

"In the potted palm."

"The palm? Were you expecting a note in the palm?" he asked.

"I was not," she said. "But I could not help opening it, you see. I know this makes me a dreadful person."

"Not at all," he said, thinking of the many, many notes and letters not addressed to him, which he had nevertheless opened.

"It said Rosetta Stone, tomorrow at noon. And my curiosity overwhelmed me. I had hoped it would be two star-crossed lovers, secretly trysting. But alas, I saw no sign of them, unless Meryton and Miss Ditherfield communicate by cryptogram, which, frankly, would surprise me. And they happened to bump into each other over by the Cracherode collection, so I cannot see how the note-exchangers could have been them. I do believe it must have been the gentlemen I overheard. They must have been the ones exchanging the note. Is that not strange?"

"Ah." He tried to sound casual. "The ones speaking of lists?"

She nodded. "Yes. They were behind me and began speaking, and did not realize I was standing so close. It is astonishing how often gentlemen discussing important things pay no mind to ladies."

Had she heard their entire exchange?

"There you are, Georgette! I feared I lost you in the horde." A young lady, all bouncy blond curls and lace and ribbons, was at Miss Quinby's side. "I must say that was all exceedingly dull. I was hoping for better from Captain James Cook."

She gave a small tug on Miss Quinby's arm. "Can we please be off? Gunter's is calling to..."

Eversley made a noise. The bouncy blonde looked over and the words died on her lips. A small squeak emerged.

He smiled. "I do not believe we have met," he said.

"Oh, do forgive me," Miss Quinby said. "Your Grace, may I please introduce my cousin, Miss Fanny Markham."

All he wanted to do was to pull Miss Quinby away from her cousin and insist she tell him what the gentlemen had been saying. Instead, he bowed.

"A pleasure, Miss Markham," he said.

Miss Markham's eyes widened. She swept a hasty curtsy. "An honor, Your Grace."

He turned to Miss Quinby. "It was a pleasure seeing you, Miss Quinby."

She smiled. "Thank you for helping me locate my cousin."

"Not at all. Might I inquire as to whether or not you are receiving visitors later today?"

He could see Miss Markham squeeze Miss Quinby's arm.

"Oh, I do not know, I..." Miss Quinby began.

"She will be," Miss Markham said. "My cousin has just received some new music and has been dying to get some time at the piano. I'd wager she will be there all afternoon. You are welcome to interrupt, Your Grace."

The Duke grinned. "Thank you, Miss Markham. I will."

5

*G*eorgette closed the door to the music room. She leaned against it and breathed a sigh of relief. Escaping Fanny had been no easy task. Her cousin had attached herself to Georgette quite aggressively, once they left the British Museum.

"Why, you little liar!" she had said to Georgette. "There you were, telling me that you and the Duke had been speaking of nothing exciting, and then you drag me off for a *tête à tête* with him in front of a slab of dead languages. I insist, you must tell me all."

Despite Georgette's many protestations, Fanny refused to believe mere coincidence had led the Duke to the museum at that hour.

"Even if I allowed for that possibility," she said, "you cannot deny that he asked to call upon you *later today*. The man is positively smitten."

Fanny would not be swayed: the Duke of Eversley was in Town after a decade of mourning, and she was determined that Georgette would be conveniently alone when he came to call.

And so now Georgette was blessedly alone, just her and Beethoven's *Sonata quasi una fantasia*.

She was so engrossed in the music that she did not realize that the Duke had entered. Finally, she ended the piece, still lost in the melody. The clapping jolted her, and she was back in the room.

"Oh!" She jumped slightly on her stool. "I did not realize you had arrived." She quickly stood and curtsied.

He stood by the door, which remained open to avoid any implications of impropriety.

"That was..." He coughed. "Quite lovely. Please, do not trouble yourself on my account. Be seated. Your cousin informed me that this was where I would find you and that, no matter how runaway with passion I might be, I must leave the door open."

Georgette smiled. "Thank you, Your Grace."

She gestured to one of the spindly, delicate chairs which were placed closer to the fire, and seated herself.

"My cousin is beside herself, believing you to be courting me. However, as she is not here, I feel I may be direct. We need not pretend you are here to be runaway with passion." She looked at him as if for permission.

He gestured for her to continue.

"I have given it some thought," she said. "What I overheard between the two gentlemen."

"Oh?" He feigned ignorance. "I had quite forgotten you overheard a conversation."

She sniffed in disbelief. He grinned.

"You have caught me out," he said. "Believe me, Miss

Quinby, when I say that if I should be on the lookout for a woman to court, I would place you at the top of the list. Nevertheless, I will admit that my purpose in coming to see you today is not romantic."

"Thank you for not playing me the fool," she said.

"Might I inquire as to what you overheard?" he asked.

"First, I must ask a question of you," she said. "Based on your behavior today, and your sudden interest in the conversation, I do believe your concern is more than passing. I simply wish to ascertain to which side your interest belongs."

He bristled visibly. "Are you suggesting I would betray my country?" he demanded. "That I would work for the country that murdered my wife? Were you a man, I would call you out."

Unless he was a truly impressive actor, that response answered her question.

"No," she said. "But you must admit that it was only right that I ask. You would no doubt do the same."

He stared at her for a long time.

"Miss Quinby," he finally said. "I do believe I regret not knowing you better before now."

She dimpled; nay, she beamed at him. "Thank you, Your Grace," she said.

"Please, call me Eversley."

"Thank you, Eversley," she said. "And now, before you lose your patience, I shall tell you what I saw and overheard. First, however, I should explain the note."

"Ah, yes, the note," he said.

"I copied it down in programme." She stood and went

over to the piano, where she riffled amongst the sheet music until she located it. She handed it to him.

He stared down at the string of numbers. "And you deciphered this?"

"There is no need to sound so astonished. It was relatively easy work, given the last word."

"Nevertheless..." He looked up. "I must admit that my astonishment is more that you believed this to be the work of romance. You must know some especially bored...trysting lovers? Was that how you put it?"

She gave him a sardonic look. "Lovers are much more common in my daily life than are traitors to the crown. Your life, I am beginning to understand, is different."

He shrugged and then looked back down at the numbers. "And you determined that it said...?"

"Rosetta Stone. Tomorrow. Noon," she said.

"Ah," he said, looking at the numbers. "The word noon must have helped hasten the solving process."

"It did." She grinned. "I thought to myself, oh, how delightful, a secret rendezvous. Little did I realize how accurate I would be. I had thought the most shocking result would be a notorious affair. Instead, as I stood, trying to locate my tragic couple, the gentlemen at my back began speaking."

She could still remember the conversation that had played out behind her. "One of the gentlemen was French. He spoke first. 'Ah, monsieur, I see you receive my little note,' he said.

The other, most certainly English, was gruffer, more belligerent in tone. 'Dash it, I haven't time for notes in ballrooms, Leclere. I told you, I expect the funds.'

'*Oui, oui*, to be assured, I am aware. We are gathering the money. But we must be discrete, *non*? You would not wish for any of it to be traced back to you, I believe. Up until now no one has traced you to be this Monsieur Lightfoot,' the Frenchman said.

'I stuck my neck out for this damned affair. Nipping that list was no easy business, I will have you know,' the Englishman said.

'*Oui, je sais.* You are ever the hero, taking a little *papier* from a desk.'

'That little *papier* is worth a king's ransom. I want the funds. If you do not deliver, I will find someone else. Many other parties would be interested in this information. Parties who are not desperately looking to sell off all their land in the Americas. And do not think you will be able to sneak in and steal it from me. You will never find it.'

There was silence for a few moments, and then a dramatic sigh.

'Do you know what this is?' the Frenchman had asked. I of course, was not able to see him, but assumed he was motioning to the slab in front of him. 'This Rosetta Stone? It is French. It should be ours. Not sitting in some disgusting museum in London. And yet, here it is.'

There was more silence and then the Frenchman spoke again. 'You will have your monies. And if you even consider selling that list to another party, you will be dead."

Georgette related the entire conversation to Eversley, attempting to capture the accents and tone of the gentlemen in question.

"That was all of it," she said to the Duke when she finished. "That was all I heard." She folded her hands in her lap.

Eversley rubbed his chin. "I can understand why you were looking so blinkered when I first saw you on the steps," he said. "Not often you overhear a conversation like that, and to remember it in such detail. You did quite well with the accents, by the way, although Merry doesn't sound so gruff, I would say."

"Mr. Meryton? Whatever do you mean?" she asked.

He had asked about Merry Meryton when he had seen her at the museum, Georgette remembered. What role did Merry play?

"Was he not the Englishman you overhead?" Eversley asked.

She thought for a moment. Had she misheard? No, she knew Merry's voice.

"I did not see their faces," Georgette said, "so I suppose I cannot speak definitively. But it certainly did not sound like Mr. Meryton. I imagine I would recognize his voice if I heard it again. I know I would recognize the Frenchman," she said.

Eversley rubbed his knees. She did not think it was Merry? But how could that be? It did not add up. Merry was believed to have taken the list. White had instructed him. Merry was the suspect. Merry was at the museum. Then Miss Quinby overhears a conversation between a man with a list and a Frenchman wanting to buy it. She had to be mistaken. It must have been Merry. Then, after his brief conversation with the Frenchman, he could have located Miss Ditherfield.

"I wish we knew when he expects the funds by," mused the Duke.

"Mmmm." She nodded. "Might I inquire about this list? What exactly is it a list of?"

He grimaced. "I'm afraid I cannot tell you that. I can tell you that it never should have been made in the first place. If I ever get my hands on it I am burning it, posthaste."

"What will you do now?" she asked.

He shrugged. "I shall continue to follow the leads that we have," he said.

He was used to the methodical drudgery of spy-work. So often, people assumed that it was excitement and swashbuckling and derring-do. More often than not, it was watching and waiting and hoping for the best. And he had been fortunate already. What a lucky break, Miss Quinby overhearing the conversation.

"I must thank you for your assistance, Miss Quinby" he said to the lady. "Your ability to break the code of the note, and to remember in such detail, the conversation which you overheard, quite impress me."

She laughed. "I suppose that is something," she said. "I must tell you, since encountering you in the garden last night; my life has become exponentially more dramatic."

"Exponentially?" he asked, quirking his eyebrow.

"Exponentially," she declared. "To the power of three, at a minimum."

"Tell me," he said, "you've revealed considerable musical and mathematical talent, and are undaunted by cryptograms. Do you have any other hidden accomplishments of which I should be aware?"

"They are not accomplishments," she said smoothly. "They are passions. Accomplishments imply that I do them for Society. Passions I do for myself."

"I stand corrected," he said. "Do you have any other passions about which I should be aware?"

The pair conversed for easily for some time. Miss Markham found them hours later, still sitting in the music room, the fire died down to embers, discussing music and mathematics and a mutual secret fondness for novels. The Duke, embarrassed by the happiness which he had felt in Miss Quinby's presence and the lightness of being, which he had experienced as they sat speaking with each other, quickly stood to take his leave.

There was an awkward moment of silence. He did not wish to go. There was nothing for him at his mansion; nothing but the ghost of his wife. James was tracking Merry, so he could not even look forward to that.

"It has been a pleasure, Miss Quinby," he said. "I hope our paths cross again."

"Yes, so do I. Do you know what is rather odd? The Rosetta Stone is not either British or French," she said. "It is Egyptian."

He laughed. "I suppose you are right," he said. "I wonder if they shall ever get it back."

Part 2

Search for a Spy

6

here was a note from James when the Duke of Eversley returned home. Merry Meryton had made his way to the gambling clubs. As it was more difficult for James to gain entry to certain hallowed establishments, footmen were generally not allowed to enter at will, Eversley set off for the clubs himself.

When he arrived at the gambling den, Merry was deep in play. He was intent on the cards, and Eversley could see the drip of perspiration trickling down the side of his forehead.

What was Merry doing? Gambling intensely, stealing lists for the French? What had happened to the jovial, happy boy he'd been at Eton and Oxford with? The Merry he knew resembled a Labrador retriever or perhaps a terrier; this Merry was more like a beaten whippet.

After watching him for some time, Eversley decided to take a seat at the table. He settled down to the game of faro, nodding at the other gentlemen there. They all stood and bowed.

"Please, gentlemen, let's not stand on ceremony." Eversley waved his hands and they sat together. Again and again, he was being reminded that he was a Duke. When he was undercover in France, the highest position he had assumed had been a wealthy merchant; more often he pretended to be a member of the criminal class. No one bowed at him in France.

And no one expected anything of him, he realized. No one wanted his thoughts on politics or farming or the state of the empire. Here, he was constantly being consulted; people were forever asking him what they should do. Had he been shirking his duties as Duke? Had he been so consumed by Blanche's death that he had forsaken the people who relied on him?

Perhaps.

"Merry, old boy, how are you?" Eversley adopted a friendly, jocular tone. "I haven't seen you in some time."

Merry wiped his brow with a handkerchief, and smiled faintly at Eversley.

"We haven't see you in Town for almost a decade," he said to the Duke. "I'd given you up."

"I dare say, I'd given myself up as well," Eversley said.

Merry nodded. "I'm terribly sorry about The Duchess," he said. "I must admit that I understand much better now what you must have gone through. Love..."

"Why, if it isn't Eversley. And Merry Meryton." Lord Fletcher gave a jocular laugh as he came over to the table. He glanced down at the cards.

"Still after your fortune, eh, Meryton?" Another laugh.

Merry colored. Lord Fletcher laughed again. He leaned in conspiratorially to Eversley.

"Our Merry here is desperate for funds," he said. "A certain lady won't wed him without them." He tapped his nose.

It was interesting, Eversley thought, how often Lord Fletcher tapped his nose. And how much he disliked the habit; and the man generally. He knew Merry was a traitor to the Crown and in possession of a list of spies for the Crown, but he found himself defending the man.

"You presume, Fletcher," he said coldly.

The man drew back, sputtering. The others at the table stared. The long-reclusive Duke of Eversley cutting Lord Fletcher? It would be on the tongues of all the gossips by morning.

Eversley closed his eyes. He should not have been so cold. He did not want gossip, especially not in an effort to help a traitor. He summoned up a smile. He would smooth this gaffe over.

"I am looking forward to the ball," he said to Fletcher, in an attempt to placate him. "Please tell her Ladyship."

Fletcher opened his mouth. His skin was mottled. Eversley wondered if he was going to tell him off.

"She will be delighted to hear that you plan to attend," he finally said. "Your tendency to avoid such events has not gone unnoticed. No doubt my lady will consider your presence a coup."

Eversley nodded. He turned back to the table and play resumed.

Fletcher wandered off shortly, much to Eversley's relief.

Merry, silent, looked down at the cards.

"It's no use," he said. "Fletcher was right to poke fun."

"How so?" Eversley asked.

"I keep thinking that perhaps miraculously I will somehow win enough, that someday I could approach Miss Ditherfield as a man of means."

"I understood Miss Ditherfield to have quite a sizable inheritance of her own," Eversley said. "Could you not simply marry her? Would that not address some of your own financial woes?"

"Certainly, but how will she know that I love her? I cannot allow her to believe that I only care for her because of her money. I cannot go to her father, seeking her hand, without having more to offer," Merry said. He mopped his brow once more.

"But what of your love for her?" Eversley asked. "Are you willing to live apart from her? To sacrifice what you might have?"

"I cannot submit her to a life less than what she deserves," Merry said.

Play continued. Eversley, through no effort of his own, watched as his winnings grew and Merry's dwindled. Why was it that the men most desperate were always the ones to lose? Why was Merry so dedicated to winning here in a gambling hall, if he was about to obtain considerable wealth from the French?

Finally, feeling vaguely ill, Eversley pushed away from the table. Merry looked up at him. Eversley put a hand on his shoulder. He wanted to tell him that Miss Ditherfield would marry him no matter the depth of his pocketbook, if she truly loved him. He wanted to tell him that no man ever found his fortunes in gambling dens. He wanted to tell him to stop making stupid choices based on pride; refusing to marry the woman as he was, always seeking more fortune. But he knew it would not be kindly received.

"Get some sleep, Merry," he said instead.

THE NEXT MORNING found Eversley seated at his breakfast table, enjoying a good steak and some breakfast tea. Joseph, another reliable footman, had been dispatched to watch over Merry's movements, which meant that Eversley had the freedom to read the paper and then begin to attend to the mountains of estate business that had amassed over the last decade.

It was in this contented state; tea, steak, and newspaper, that his sister and her husband found him.

"Charles." Judith bent down to present her cheek for a kiss and then settled into a chair. "Imagine my surprise, learning you were in town."

Lady Judith, Eversley's younger sister, was a beautiful woman. She was tall and regal, with golden hair and a strong nose. Her eyes were green and very beautiful, although all too frequently they were narrowed, which lessened their effect somewhat. Today, she wore a fine *pelisse*, decorated with a Greek key pattern. Judith had never worn anything but that which was all the rage.

Eversley nodded to Sebastien and offered him tea. He had not seen his friend for many years. Sebastien looked much the same. Handsome and dashing, with a lock of hair falling artistically in the middle of his forehead. His clothing was fine, a single-breasted morning coat in green, and his Hessians boots were impressively shined.

"To what do I owe the pleasure of your visit?" Eversley asked "Not that you need ever have a reason, my dear sister. I merely wonder as to your attendance at my breakfast table." He reached for the marmalade. "I never knew you to be an early riser."

"To what indeed?" Judith laughed. "Do you know, we heard the most ridiculous rumor last night, when we were at Vauxhall? I positively lost my breath, did I not, Sebastien?"

"Indeed, you did, my dear. I do not know when I last saw you so shocked."

For a moment, Eversley nearly dropped his knife. Surely Meryton had not spread about rumors as to the names on the list? What if everyone became aware about his secret activities over the last decade? His mouth grew dry. If it came out that he was a spy, many peoples' lives in France would be at stake. He had spent years developing friends and networks.

"In the past two days, you have been seen twice in the company of Miss Georgette Quinby," his sister said. "Twice," she repeated.

Eversley hid a sigh of relief by attacking his steak; he had not been exposed as a spy. So, this was about Miss Quinby. He should not have been surprised. No doubt the gossips had gone mad over his interactions with the former fiancé of his sister's husband.

"And there's been suggestion of a third time," Sebastien added. "A visit to her home."

Goodness, the gossips were certainly busy. Then again, he had not bothered to hide his visit. Why should he?

"Miss. Georgette. Quinby." His sister stabbed her finely gloved finger on the table to punctuate each word. "You cannot mean to be interested in her, brother."

He was not romantically interested in Miss Quinby. But his sister's attitude rankled.

"Why should I not be interested in Miss Quinby?" he asked sipping his tea.

"Have you been beggared?" Sebastien asked. He smiled as if that would be a fun joke. Eversley supposed it would be ironic, given the amount of money he had given to the two of them over the years.

"Did you lose some excessive amount of funds?" Judith asked, her brow furrowed as if she had not considered such a disaster.

"No, I remain as wealthy as ever," he said, calmly.

"Did your injury from fox hunting also affect your brain?" she asked.

He had told his sister that his wound had been the result of a fall from a horse. She was still ignorant as to his presence in France over the past decade. She believed he had spent the years holed up in one of his estates in the North.

"No," he said. "None of those things."

"Then what in heaven's name are you doing with Miss Quinby?" she demanded.

He set his cup down. "Miss Quinby is quite enjoyable company," he said.

"Miss Quinby is a spoiled heiress," Sebastien said.

"Was," Eversley said. He was beginning to feel almost angry. "She *was* a spoiled heiress, and even that statement could be up for debate. She was sixteen and she adored you."

"She tried to steal Sebastian from me!" Judith said.

"Is that how it happened? I thought she was engaged to Sebastien," he said, looking to his friend for confirmation.

Sebastien sighed and nodded his head. He might be relatively devoid of character, but he did tend to admit the truth.

"And you, dear sister, decided to take him from *her*," Eversley said.

"She did not deserve him," Judith said. She threw Sebastien a look of adoration. He patted her hand.

"That may well be," Eversley said. "I am inclined to believe that the two of you deserve each other far more. But that certainly is no reason for me to not associate with her."

Judith snorted. "My dear brother, if you are eager to find a lady, I am happy to assist you. Surely you can do better than her. I have many friends who are eligible young ladies. I would be happy to introduce you. Indeed it is time, you set about finding wife. The Dukedom requires an heir."

"Yes, but I find I do not wish to set about finding a wife. I had one, lest you forgot. And I loved her. While you might so easily forget Blanche, I do not."

"I did not mean..." Judith began.

He stood, cutting her off.

"I am suddenly tired, Judith. Nor do I care to have this

conversation again. As far as I can tell, you won your husband with absolutely no consideration of the heart or sentiments of the young lady to whom he was engaged."

He turned to Sebastien.

"And you, my dear friend, led her to believe you loved her. Perhaps the both of you are feeling guilt due to ruining her life, and this is why you speak of her in such terms; it is a defensive gesture. Whatever it may be, I am in no mood to entertain it. I enjoy Miss Quinby's company, and I intend to continue enjoying it. We are friends."

"But you're a duke," Judith sputtered. "You cannot go about becoming friends with common spinsters."

"You are a duke's daughter, Judith," Eversley said. "I have seen no indication that that has instilled in you any sort of manners. Why should I not be friends with common spinsters of enjoyable conversation?"

Judith, already waspish, opened her mouth to retort.

"Judith," Sebastien said. He laid a hand on her arm. "Let us not bicker with your brother. I believe we should be glad Eversley is out and enjoying Town."

He looked at Eversley. "It is good to have you back, old boy."

7

*I*t was cruel, Georgette thought, how something could happen in one's life to make it suddenly full of color and excitement, and then that color would disappear as abruptly as it began. She always felt alive, to be sure. One of her resolutions following her heartbreak, when she was younger, was to always appreciate the life she woke up to. But it seemed especially cruel to spend time helping a duke engaged in espionage and service to the Crown on day, and then be left to stare at droplets running down window panes the next.

The days following the moment at the British museum, and the Duke's subsequent visit, were marked by foul weather. Georgette and Fanny had been primarily restricted to the indoors, being outside only to travel from the door of their townhome to the covered safety of the carriage. Not wanting to trouble the servants, they had limited their activities outside the home to only the very necessary outings.

This had meant that the two of them had spent an excessive amount of time in each other's company. They had embroidered. They had played cards. They had read aloud to each other. They had read in silence. Fanny had modeled and Georgette had drawn her. Georgette had played the piano and Fanny had sung. They began the whole sequence again with embroidery, and cards.

On the morning of yet another dreary day, Fanny bounded into the breakfast room.

"This was just delivered," she said. She placed a package at Georgette's elbow.

"Whatever could it be?" Georgette tore it open.

It was a packet of music with a note.

I quite enjoyed our discussion several days ago. I thought you might appreciate some new music to play, to liven any boredom you might be feeling due to the icy rain and wind. I hope to see you again soon.

Yrs. Eversley

"He sent you a piano arrangement of Beethoven's ballet." Fanny was thumbing through the music while Georgette read the note. "Heavens, he must like you even more than I originally believed."

"He does not..."

Fanny held up a staying hand. "No," she said. "No, you will not persuade me. This is enough." She snatched the note out of Georgette's hand and read it. Then she lifted an eyebrow, daring Georgette to say that the Duke was not interested in her romantically. Which he was not, Georgette knew, but she understood that Fanny was not to be swayed.

"I would like you to know that I am all in favor of this match, dear cousin," Fanny said. "If you become a duchess, my own chances of a good match greatly improve. You could at least entertain the man's affection. For me. After all, up until this point, you've been a bit of a burden. You know it is true. I have no hopes of getting into Almack's at the moment, but that would all change if you married the Duke of Eversley." She batted her eyes pleadingly in Georgette's direction. "Please, cousin. For me?"

"Oh, be off with you." Georgette swatted Fanny with the music. "Find someone else to bother. Perhaps Mrs. Timms, the housekeeper, knows a viscount."

Her cousin, laughing gleefully, left the room.

Georgette sat back down at the piano. What a delight! New music. She began to pick out the melody. He hoped to see her again. If she did see him, what should she say to him? What should she do? Should she send him a reply; a note of thanks?

Goodness, she had not been so excited to receive something from a gentleman since...her fingers faltered on the keys.

Since Sebastien.

No, she would not allow it. This time it was different. She was a grown woman now. She knew that the Duke was not interested in her, no matter what Fanny might say. He had loved his wife. That was it. He had loved

Blanche with all of his heart and then she died and he would never love again.

He had told her this.

She had sworn she would never love another as well. Georgette had sworn to herself that never again would she set her heart out on a platter for someone to destroy. Never again would she risk her pride, her vanity, her sense of self, for a man.

She had told him this. It was true.

Then why was she thinking about him? Wondering what this gesture meant? She knew what it meant. He enjoyed her company. They were two survivors, of a fashion and he had respected her accidental involvement in his work.

She liked to think she had impressed him with her ability to easily break the code of the cypher note, and to remember the conversation between the two gentlemen at the museum. Perhaps they were friends. They could be that. If they were friends her heart would not be in such trouble. His friendship would lift her spirits.

She should pen him a note. She wished she could deduce if he had learned anything more regarding the list. What was it a list of? How could a list be so valuable? Her curiosity was working overtime. Could Mr. Meryton really be involved? He seemed so certain it had been Merry whom she overheard, but Georgette knew Merry. His cousin was the same age as she was, and they had made their debut together. Merry was the type of gentleman on whom one could always rely; he danced with all the girls, wallflowers and diamonds alike. Merry would not work with the French. Merry would not betray his country.

The Englishman who had spoken had been more unpleasant. She believed she would recognize his voice if she heard it again, but could not be certain. Similarly with the Frenchman. Not that she had any opportunities to overhear voices, given the weather. Unless the Frenchman had hidden in her kitchen as the errand boy, she would not find them here.

She sighed. It was cruel, being exposed to some excitement, only to have it taken away. The Duke was sending her the music to be polite; he did not have any interest in her, as a friend or anything more.

THE FOLLOWING AFTERNOON, the gloomy skies had finally cleared. A fact which Fanny announced brightly to Georgette.

"We are going riding," she said with a tone that brooked no argument and the two of women hastened to Hyde Park. Fanny insisted they don their finest carriage-riding attire and they both looked quite smart, bedecked in ribboned bonnets and lambswool *pelisses*, half boots, and kid gloves.

Although it was no longer raining ice, and a reluctant sun peered from between the clouds, the London streets were muddy disasters. The carriage lurched along, and Georgette could not help feeling sympathy for the poor horses.

Once they hit the gravel of Hyde Park, however,

conditions improved slightly. The vast expanse of green, crossed with riding trails and larger paths for carriages, was the place to see and be seen.

The rest of the *Ton* evidently had the same idea, for the park was packed to the gills with carriages and ladies and gentlemen on horseback.

The two ladies, and Swindon, their excellent driver, made their way to the Ring. As they went along, they exchanged pleasantries with a number of other ladies and gentlemen.

"I cannot help noticing that we appear to be popular items," Fanny said. "No doubt we have your ducal attentions to thank for that."

Georgette rolled her eyes, but it was true: more and more people seemed eager to pause to chat with them. It was odd, Georgette thought. For years she had submitted to snubs and the lack of invitations. She had accepted this as her due for her hysterical behavior as a young lady. Now, however, she had been seen in the company of a duke, a mysterious duke, at that and suddenly everyone wished to speak with her.

"Oh, goodness, the gossips are going to go mad for this," Fanny said.

Georgette looked at her. "What are you on about?" she asked.

"Something wicked this way comes," Fanny said, her eyes glittering.

Georgette looked around and her stomach suddenly sank to the soles of her beautiful half boots.

"Perhaps they will not see us," she said quietly to Fanny.

Fanny snorted.

Lady Judith and her Adonis of a husband, Lord Sebastien Falks, pulled alongside the carriage.

"Well, well, well," Lady Judith said. "If it isn't The Mad Heiress."

Georgette swallowed. She wanted to shrink away into nothing, float off into the clouds above Hyde Park. Lady Judith had always intimidated her, even before she had run off with Sebastien. It was as if part of her had always known, Georgette thought, that Lady Judith wanted Sebastien to be hers. She had certainly stared plenty of daggers at Georgette when they were both young ladies. Georgette could still remember it: Lady Judith was forever glowering at her from the sides of ballrooms and assemblies and picnics and outings. Perhaps that was why Blanche, the Duchess of Eversley had been so nice to her, to compensate for the ever-poor behavior of her sister-in-law.

She took a deep breath. No. She would not let the lady continue to haunt her. Lady Judith had already won. Georgette would not allow her the satisfaction of seeing her squirm now.

"Lord and Lady Falks." She pasted a false smile on her face. "How lovely to see you."

Lady Judith laughed. "I wish I could say the same thing to you, Miss Quinby. I must say, your audacity astonishes me."

"My audacity?"

"Indeed. Chivvying after my brother. I would ask if you had any pride at all, but I already know you don't," Lady Judith said. "You must know that any attention he

69

gives you is due to his soft heart. He would never seriously consider you. He simply would not like for you to be further embarrassed in front of the *Ton* by any sort of public rejection from him."

Yes, Georgette did know this, but it hurt to hear it from the lady who had already ruined her life. Before she could answer—indeed, what would she say? Fanny turned to Georgette to ask her, "Is she always so unpleasant?"

"I do not know how she conducts herself with other people," Georgette hedged. "But yes, with me, she is."

"I will not bother to ask who this is," Lady Judith said. "Gossip has already informed me that you are in Town to bring out your cousin." She looked Fanny up and down. "Good luck," she said to Fanny. "You certainly will need it."

"I have no doubt that Fanny will do extraordinarily well," Georgette said. "She is rare, for someone so young. She knows what she wants, and she understands when the people around her merely pretend to be willing to give it to her." She looked at Sebastien. "Fanny would never make the mistake of giving her heart to someone who failed to value it."

For a moment Sebastien looked at her. She could see it. And she realized he had never really looked at her. When they were engaged, his eyes had always slid away from her, or glazed over, or drifted away. For just a moment, he looked at her, and saw her, and then he looked away.

She had spoken the truth. She knew Fanny would not make the mistake she had made. And she had made it. She had been so overjoyed that such a handsome man, and a lord to boot, wanted to marry her. She had created an entire fictional version of him in her head. In her dreams, Sebastien had seen her and fallen immediately in love. It was Romeo and Juliet, only they were not star-crossed. Nonetheless, she had treated him as her Romeo, only she was not his Juliet. She was Rosaline, left behind, and forgotten, but alive. He should not have broken her heart, but she should not have given it to him. She had given it to a mirage, to a man who existed only in her dreams.

"Drive on, Sebastien." Lady Judith gave her one last glare. Lord Falks blinked, shook his head, and flicked the reins.

"Well!" Fanny turned to her. "We are sure to be the topic of many supper conversations this evening."

Georgette looked out. Several members of society were staring blatantly, curiously back. She smiled at them until her face began to ache.

"Yes, I suppose we are," she said.

8

*H*e should not have sent the music. Eversley did not know what had compelled him to do such a thing. It felt right. Miss Quinby had been playing Beethoven's sonata when he visited a week ago, and she had looked so lovely. And then her eyes had glowed as she spoke of Beethoven's music. And he had told her about seeing Beethoven's new ballet in Vienna last year. And...and.... and what? He sighed.

He had not told her that he had been in Vienna because he was recovering from a near mortal stabbing he had suffered in France, shortly after the Peace of Amiens. However, he could not shake the overwhelming feeling that he would share those details with her at some later date, and she would understand.

Ridiculous. This was ridiculous. He had first seen her in the garden a week ago. He barely knew the lady. He certainly had not gained a good measure of her when she had been a chit barely out of the schoolroom and engaged to his friend Sebastien, but now he felt as if he had known her for years.

She was a friend. That was it. She was a friend and he had not had a good friend for so long. After Blanche, those with whom he had been close had drifted, or been pushed, away. He no longer confided in people. It was a drawback of his work as a spy. He had learned not to trust, not to confide.

But he wanted to confide in Miss Quinby. He wanted to tell her about being stabbed in France. He wanted to tell her the burdens he bore for his country. He wanted to tell her about the contents of the list and the people on it; people who depended upon him. He wanted to tell her about what he had done for England. He wanted to tell her about realizing how he had shirked his responsibilities as Duke. He wanted to tell her about his day, just his day.

There was no reason he could not do this, he realized. They could be friends. He had sworn to never again fall in love; he hadn't sworn to never again have a dear friend in whom he could confide.

She was nothing like Blanche. Blanche had always been so cool, so elegant, so beautiful. Georgette was quicksilver and passionate, but Blanche had liked her, even all those years ago, and he had never known Blanche to be wrong about a person, save once, when she went back to France for her family. Even then, she went to persuade them to come to England. She was right even then. She was right; only she was too late.

Oh, Blanche. What am I doing?

The ghost of his wife stood in the room with him,

watching him tie his cravat, her ethereal form gazing at him. She was wearing powder. It was such a little thing, he thought, to realize that when she had last stood, living, in his dressing room, they had both dusted their hair. He had not worn powder for years. Where had the time gone?

"Sending music to a lady," she said. "I do believe you might have a little *tendre*."

He shook his head, trying to shake the vision of her away, trying to refuse her accusation. She walked forward, reaching out to him, trying to touch his cheek.

"I like her," she said. "Your *mademoiselle*."

"She is not my *mademoiselle*," he said. "Although I do believe she might become my friend."

Blanche smiled. "That is good," she said. "You need a friend."

Then she was gone, vanished, nothing but a breath of wind against his cheek. He was alone in his dressing room with no one but his valet, who was eyeing him with some misgiving.

He finished tying his cravat, and allowed his valet to brush his shoulders. He had learned yesterday evening, during his now regular visit to the gambling halls to keep an eye on Merry, that his sister had taunted Miss Quinby in Hyde Park. The word was that Judith had accused Miss Quinby of "chivvying" after him.

Miss Quinby did not strike him as such. She did not have lures; she did not try to bring him in or give chase.

He was irked with his sister. She had always been spoilt and rude. Blanche had never admitted to disliking her, but neither had she ever expressed any interest in spending time with Judith. When Sebastien had run off to Gretna with her, he had been relieved. His sister, and all her tantrums and fits and mean-spirited remarks, would now be Sebastien's problem, not his.

Still, he found himself unable to let her reported behavior to Miss Quinby go unchecked. Judith had already ruined Miss Quinby's life. Did she need to confront her in public as well? It seemed terribly mean-spirited. There was no point.

On a whim, he had invited Miss Quinby and her cousin to a small supper and musicale performance which was to be held at the house of an old friend. He knew that Stewart would not mind the addition of two ladies at the last moment, and he wanted Judith to know that he would continue to associate with Miss Quinby, no matter how horribly his sister might behave.

Eversley's note, inviting the ladies, had been dispatched this morning. The acceptance, penned by Miss Markham, had arrived soon after. They would be happy to attend a musicale, and would await his escort.

For the first time in many many years, Eversley found himself dressing up for a lady.

9

_G_eorgette could not believe Fanny had accepted the Duke's invitation without asking her. She had returned from a visit to the Hatchard's and been told by her cousin that the Duke had invited them to dine and enjoy a musicale performance at Lord Stewart's, this very evening.

"Heavens," Georgette had said. "I do not know that we should go."

"Certainly we must," Fanny had said. "And we will, for I have already accepted."

Georgette grumbled quite loudly, but secretly she was pleased. He had invited them! Her spirts lifted, and her heart pattered like a butterfly against her chest. It was silly. They were only friends. Indeed, he was probably just being polite.

She assumed that his actions were prompted by what had occurred in Hyde Park the day before. He should not feel any obligation to befriend her. The actions of his sister did not reflect on him, and yet she was happy that he had made the gesture. She wanted to see him.

She took extra care with dressing. Her gown was white satin, trimmed with green velvet, her stomacher heavily ornamented. Her brown hair was elaborately done into a pile of curls. Fanny burst into her dressing room as the maid was helping her pull on her gloves.

"Oh, don't you look a treat," Fanny said. "The Duke is sure to fall even more in love with you."

"The Duke is not falling in love with me to begin with," Georgette said, calmly.

"Pish posh." Fanny waved her gloved arms about. "Nevertheless, you do look lovely."

"As do you," Georgette said. Her cousin was more demurely dressed; fitting for the younger lady, but the rose of her gown flattered her coloring and her golden curls. The ribbon strung through her curls matched her dress.

"I have been told he is here," Fanny said, eagerly. "Which is quite a relief, I must say. There is nothing worse than dressing and waiting, unable to sit for fear one's gown will wrinkle."

"Indeed," Georgette said dryly. "Nothing worse."

Fanny took her arm, and the two of them made their way down the stairs to where the Duke awaited them.

Georgette's heart gave a small twinge when she saw him. He was so handsome, dressed in a coat of superfine, and well-fitting breeches. He looked up at the ladies as they descended, then bowed.

"The two of you lovely ladies put me to shame," he said.

Georgette dimpled. It was so nice to be attended. She allowed him to bow again and kiss her hand. He then made the same motions to Fanny.

He motioned to the door. "Shall we?" he asked. "My carriage awaits."

The party made their way to the carriage and climbed in.

"How extraordinary," Fanny said, once they had settled into the carriage.

"Oh?" The Duke sounded confused. "May I ask what is extraordinary?"

"I assumed a duke's carriage would be bedecked in leather and jewels. But it isn't. It looks just like our carriage."

Georgette watched as he bit back a smile. "I must apologize. I recently arrived in London. I have not yet had time to properly outfit my carriage."

Fanny nodded seriously. "No doubt you have had other thoughts on your mind. Such as Georgette."

For a moment his eyes widened in surprise, then quickly shuttered.

"Er, yes," he said to Fanny. He glanced over at Miss Quinby.

She cast her eyes heavenward. His lips quirked, and the tension in her stomach loosened. He knew she did not believe him to be avidly courting her. Fanny would no doubt be disappointed when no romance would result, but Georgette was glad to know that the Duke did not believe her to be laboring under any misapprehensions.

"The musical performance is to be at Lord Stewart's house?" Georgette asked.

"It is," he said. "Stewart always has extremely accomplished performers. I hope you will enjoy yourselves."

"I've no doubt we shall."

EVERSLEY KEPT BEING SURPRISED by how pretty Miss Quinby was. Throughout the evening, whenever he glanced over towards the lady, he felt as if he was noticing some new detail.

The way she dimpled when her cousin leaned in to speak to her; the way she cocked her head to listen to the music; the way she patiently stood next to Lady Fitzravels, as the lady related her health concerns in detail.

He should save her, he thought, from Lady Fitzravels. It was the gentlemanly thing to do. He made his way across the room, and navigated Miss Quinby away from the old dowager.

After Miss Quinby thanked him for rescuing her from the conversation, she turned their talk to his gift of the music. She had been practicing it daily, and hoped that at some point he would allow her to play it for him.

"It will not compare to the performance you saw in Vienna, I've no doubt of that," she said. "But it would bring me joy, to share it with you."

He assured her that he would greatly enjoy hearing her play.

They made their way to one of the quieter corners of the room. The musical entertainment had been quite enjoyable, and the guests were enjoying refreshments and conversation.

"I must inquire, whether there has been any development since last week." Her eyes darted back and forth. "Regarding the, um, what I overheard."

He bit his tongue. Her attempt at subtlety was adorable.

"Unfortunately, I have nothing new to report," he said.

"Oh." She looked so disappointed.

He wanted to wipe that look off her face, to make her smile again.

"But there is something that you might assist me with," he said.

Her eyes were so bright when she was excited, he thought. She leaned forward conspiratorially.

"What might that be?" she whispered.

He bent down slightly. He could smell the scent of her...was it perfume? Blanche had worn a discrete perfume that smelled like wisteria. Miss Quinby smelled more like strawberries. Was that possible?

"I need to do something that might possibly be considered unlawful," he said.

"Unlawful?"

"I need to search a man's living quarters," he said.

"Without his permission?"

"Yes."

"I know you are a duke, but there is no question. That is most certainly unlawful," she said.

He shrugged. "I suppose that means you do not wish to help. Forget I said anything."

She looked at him with a gimlet eye.

"What is it you would ask me to do?" she asked.

"I need the gentleman in question to be distracted for some time," he said.

She raised an eyebrow. "Mr. Meryton?"

He nodded.

She breathed out in exasperation. "I told you it was not Mr. Meryton. I know Merry."

"Be that as it may, I am operating on additional information. I ask you to trust me."

She chewed her lip. "Very well," she said. "I maintain that it was another gentleman, but I will trust you. So long as you promise to trust me, if I ever determine who that gentleman was."

He bowed in agreement. "Do you know how you might be able to distract Merry for the duration of an afternoon?" he asked.

She chewed her lip again and then nodded. "Yes," she said.

"Yes?"

He looked at her. She dimpled at him.

"But I shan't tell you," she said.

He growled slightly in exasperation. She laughed.

"When were you hoping to search his rooms?" she asked.

"As soon as I might," he said

She nodded. "Tomorrow afternoon," she said. "I shall send a footman to tell you, once the coast is clear."

He opened his mouth and closed it. "Tomorrow afternoon? So soon?"

"Do you doubt me?" she asked in a teasing tone.

"I am astonished," he said. "How are you so certain?"

"It is my secret," she said. "In return, however, I request a favor. Would you be willing to escort Fanny and me to the Castleton ball the following evening?"

"Happily. But you truly will not tell me?"

"I shall not. That will be your punishment, for continuing to believe it might be Mr. Meryton. Now, you must speak to other ladies. People are beginning to stare."

"Are you embarrassed to be seen with a duke?" he asked.

She laughed. He wanted to draw out her laughs all night.

"Not embarrassed, no. But I do believe that people other than Fanny will begin to misinterpret your interest if we continue to speak in a corner. They may not be so ready to believe that we are merely friends."

"Friends. That is what we are, is it not?" he asked.

"Yes," she said. "I believe we might become very good friends. I feel great promise in the future."

He smiled.

She wished to be friends with him. Good.

10

*G*eorgette went in search of Fanny the next morning. "We are escorting Delia Ditherfield later this afternoon, are we not?"

Fanny groaned. "Oh, lud, I'd forgotten. Could we possibly send our regrets? It is not that I don't adore Delia, for I do. I simply do not know how much more of this I can take. Why can she not marry Mr. Meryton and be done with it?"

"I was under the impression that they were not yet betrothed," Georgette said.

"They are not, it is true, although it continues to astonish me. What are they waiting for?" Fanny blew a stray curl away from her eyes.

Delia Ditherfield and Fanny had become friends the previous year. Both heiresses, the two young ladies had bonded over the difficulties associated with being in possession of a great deal of money, and the courtship struggles that come with it. Fanny, ever cautious after witnessing Georgette's heartbreak a decade earlier, maintained constant distance from the gentlemen interested in her. Thus far, into her second season, she had not demonstrated any particular interest in any of the young men who buzzed about. Delia, on the other hand, had fallen madly in love with Merry Meryton the previous year. He had been very reserved around her, however. This action Georgette had attributed to his hesitation to court an heiress, when he had very little funds himself. Georgette believed that Merry, ever affable and friendly, also possessed a considerable amount of pride, which prevented him from feeling he could extend an offer of marriage to a woman when he had so little to offer her, other than his heart.

This knowledge of the situation with Delia, was one of the reasons she refused to believe Merry could be a traitor to the Crown. However, it was also one of the reasons why she felt compelled to admit that he might be. Could he be driven to commit such a heinous act, out of love for Delia? Georgette believed no; Merry operated on a very transparent and identifiable code of gentlemanly conduct: do not offer for a woman unless you have the means of supporting her; do not compromise her virtue; do not betray your country.

She did have to admit that she had derived a particular sort of glee when Eversley had asked her to somehow distract Mr. Meryton for an afternoon. She had been about to refuse, to say she wanted no part in the activity, when she remembered that Fanny had already agreed to escort Delia to Gunter's, where Merry would meet them. The Duke's very evident admiration of her ability to lure Merry away, despite not knowing that she was in fact doing nothing out of the ordinary, had been extremely gratifying.

Fanny, however, was unaware that the Duke of Eversley was hoping to break into Merry Meryton's rooms to search for a special list, and so the afternoon for her was less than thrilling. Both Delia and Merry had an unfortunate tendency to ignore all other company when in the presence of each other which made them less than pleasant companions. They had eyes only for each other.

"Cheer up," she told Fanny. "After ices perhaps we can stop to buy some ribbons. Eversley has agreed to accompany us to the Castleton ball on the morrow. Therefore, you must look very fine."

Fanny gasped. "You sly minx," she said. "Have you done with denying he is courting you?"

"I have not. We are good friends, nothing more. Accept what it is, Fanny, do not push for more than it can be."

THE DUKE OF EVERSLEY had broken into more apartments than he would care to admit. This activity, he had justified because he was doing work for his country, for his nation, his sovereign, and, most importantly, to avenge Blanche's death. He had broken into mansions filled with spies, tents in a French bivouac, underground apartments hiding French nobility who had escaped the mobs, even Napoleon's own quarters.

Therefore, searching Merry's apartments was

relatively child's play. He dispatched James to follow Meryton himself, and Joseph to distract his manservant. He had lifted Meryton's key and done a wax pressing earlier in the week. That afternoon, dressed in the uniform and wig of a manservant, he made his way to the Albany.

He had chosen the afternoon, as it was the time when most of the gentlemen were bound to be out. It was also the time for errands and visitors, and therefore no one looked amiss at a manservant with a key.

The Albany on Picadilly had been converted into apartments the previous year. The stately former townhome belonging to the Duke of York boasted a courtyard flanked by outbuildings. The front door which was grand, yet not overly so, was accessed up a small flight of steps from the ever-bustling courtyard.

The address had become the most popular among bachelors in Town. It had also provided a solution to some of the more impoverished gentry. Based on his inquiries, Eversley knew that Merry was able to let his townhome to a merchant family, and take much smaller quarters at the Albany. It also allowed him to let go of most of his staff.

Still, many of the other gentlemen residents had a good deal of staff, who accessed the building via the back. It was through this entrance that Eversley made his way that afternoon. He had previously entered the house several times in this costume, partly to ensure that he could locate Meryton's suite without trouble, but also to allow enough of the other staff to recognize him, and to therefore not believe anything was amiss.

The entire effort went smoothly. He quickly entered the apartments, which were almost painfully bare. Meryton must have left most of the furniture in his townhome, or been forced to sell it. Eversley methodically worked his way through the rooms, tapping walls and floorboards, checking under furniture and drawers. Once, he believed he had located a promising space, but it merely resulted in a cache of love letters.

Delia Ditherfield. Goodness, the man was smitten. Hastily, Eversley returned the letters to their hiding place, not wanting to invade his friend's romantic privacy.

Eversley did not understand. If Merry needed money, why not simply marry Miss Ditherfield. Did her father threaten to withhold her inheritance if she married Meryton? He shouldn't. Merry came from an old and established family. He was also well known as a good and kind gentleman, whose family wealth had been destroyed by the previous generation's excess, not his own. He was a good man.

Aside from being a possible spy for France and a traitor to the Crown, that was.

But there was no evidence that Merry was a traitor to the Crown; at least, not in this apartment. Eversley gave it one final sweep and then, shaking his head, departed the apartment and the Albany.

He cut back towards his mansion in Mayfair, pondering what to do next. He could not say he was surprised that he did not discover anything in Meryton's apartments. Something about this entire assignment felt wrong. He chewed the inside of his lip as he ran over the details. Meryton was one of the suspects who could have taken the list. Meryton had no funds. He was in love with Miss Ditherfield, but refused to offer for her out of some sense of ego and pride.

But if Merry had the list, he would know the people on the list.

He would know the people on the list.

Eversley stopped abruptly in the middle of the street.

"Oi! Watch where ye be going!" a woman with a large basket yelled at him as she passed.

Eversley blinked at her. He looked around. Everywhere, men and women were passing him. Tradesmen, servants, street sellers, lightskirts, all of them with somewhere to be. He had forgotten how exhilarating London was. Paris had been similar, but also so very different, and so filled with mistrust and apprehension for the future.

Merry would know that Eversley was a spy, and yet, he had betrayed no nervousness in Eversley's presence. He had not deviated from his routine. He had accepted Eversley's attention as that of a friend. While it was very possible that Merry was truly that incredible of an actor, Eversley doubted it.

Miss Quinby was in the right. The spy could not be Merry.

11

Fanny sighed, untied her bonnet and tossed it carelessly onto the divan. "Oh, Thank heavens that is ended."

Georgette had to admit it had been somewhat excruciating. Merry Meryton and Delia Ditherfield had eyes for no other when in each other's presences. She and Fanny had been superfluous, window dressing, necessary only to keep society from undue gossip.

Merry and Delia had visited over ices for as long as they possibly could. Finally, the gentleman had taken his leave, and Georgette, Fanny, and Delia had returned to their carriage, where Delia had promptly burst into tears.

"I simply do not understand," she had wept into her handkerchief. "Why will Merry not ask me to be his wife?"

"I believe Mr. Meryton does not feel he deserves to ask you to be his wife," Georgette said.

"But why?" Delia had wailed. "I have repeatedly

attempted to tell him that I do not object to his family's poverty."

"Did you say it in quite that manner?" Fanny asked.

"What do you mean?" Delia sniffed.

"Simply that I have never met a man who enjoys being told that, despite his very pointed inadequacy, you love him nonetheless."

Georgette raised an eyebrow at Fanny. "Have you told a gentleman that you love him despite his very evident inadequacy? Are you speaking from experience, cousin."

Fanny merely fixed Georgette with a look. "Do I look like someone who would fall in love with a gentleman with an inadequacy?"

Georgette grinned. "No, I must admit, you do not."

Delia had then sobbed some more. Her tears were mostly dried by the time the carriage dropped her off at her family's townhome, but both Georgette and Fanny were feeling somewhat overwhelmed.

"Ahem." It was the butler.

"Yes, Smith?" Georgette asked.

"There is a manservant here to speak with you, Miss Quinby. I placed him in the yellow room."

"A manservant? Whose manservant?"

"The Duke of Eversley, Miss."

Fanny raised her eyebrows and then her hand. "The Duke of Eversley is just Miss Quinby's friend, Smith. You mustn't get excited."

"No, Miss." The butler, well acquainted with Fanny's informality, stood stoically next to the door as Georgette passed by.

She entered the yellow room. The manservant was

standing in the middle of the room. His coat and trousers did not fit him perfectly, and his wig was askew. He looked slightly awkward.

But familiar. He looked familiar.

Georgette stopped and looked him up and down. Then quickly walked forward.

"Heavens, Eversley," she said. "Do you often call upon ladies, dressed as a manservant?"

He grinned, suddenly looking decades younger, despite the wig.

"Did I fool you at all?" he asked. "Was there even a moment of doubt?"

"A moment," she conceded. "You might have fooled me better had I not known whose manservant you were purporting to be."

"I have many manservants," he said.

"To be sure, but not that many who would visit me. May I ask the reason for the costume?"

"Lest you forget, I was doing a small amount of reconnaissance. This particular uniform allows me a shocking amount of liberty. No one notices a manservant."

"You are incredibly knowledgeable about this. Are your espionage activities always so thorough?"

"Not always. On occasion they are positively dull."

She burst out laughing. "I find that difficult to imagine," she said. "I do not believe anything you could do would ever be dull."

He had frozen, as if suffering from some sort of blow. He was staring at her intently. She suddenly felt awkward. She traced a finger over the top of one of the chairs and swallowed.

He cleared his throat.

"Believe me," he said. "Dull beyond belief. One time I had to sit at a wharf, waiting for a ship to come in."

"That does not sound very dull. It sounds exciting. Sea breeze, sailors, possibly pirates. Oh dear!"

"I had to wait there for a month."

"You exaggerate."

He placed his hands over his heart. "I swear it," he said, staring soulfully into her eyes.

She smiled. "Did you find anything from your possibly unlawful activities?"

He cleared his throat. "Only that Merry Meryton is extremely attached to Delia Ditherfield."

She nodded. "So.You admit then that Merry is not the Englishman I overheard."

He rubbed his jaw. "I admit that it was likely someone else," he said. "Will that do?"

"I suppose it must," she said.

"Will you tell me now how you managed to lure Merry out?" he asked.

"Oh. He already had an appointment with Delia for ices. Fanny and I were escorts to alleviate the gossip. It has been planned for over a week."

"So, you did nothing. You led me to believe you had a brilliant plan of attack, when in reality you simply went about your day as already planned."

"I ensured he did not leave too soon. That must count for something." Her eyes twinkled mischievously.

"No doubt that was incredibly difficult, ensuring that

he did not pry himself away from his beloved too quickly."

"You have no idea," she said. She placed her clasped hands beneath her chin and looked up at him through her lashes. "Oh, Merry!"

Playing along, he took one of her hands and held it over her heart.

"Oh, my love!" he said.

She giggled, and they stared at each other. At first, in fun; playing at being Merry and Delia, staring soulfully into each other's eyes. But then his eyes turned searching, flitting to the corner's of her face, down to her lips, back up to her eyes.

She coughed delicately and looked away, breaking the spell.

He let his hand fall to his side.

"Tell me," he said. "Did Sebastien ever declare his love for you?"

Sebastien? Why was he asking about Sebastien? She could not think of Sebastien now.

"Um." She tried to gather her thoughts. "Do you mean did he ever say that he loved me?"

He nodded.

She thought back, all those years ago.

"No," she said. "He was at least that honorable. He told me I would make him the happiest of men if I accepted his offer of marriage. He called me his dearest. He snuck kisses in the garden and flattered my beauty, my intelligence, my taste. But no, he never told me he loved me.

That did not much matter to me at seventeen,

however. I created a version of Sebastien in my mind, and he told me how much he loved me, every day. In the end that was part of what so undid me. To realize that the man in my mind was so very different from the true flesh-and-blood man; it unmoored me."

He nodded. "I hate to say it, but I am relieved that my friend at least never said that he loved you. That seems an especially cruel lie."

She smiled, sadly. "It was an excellent lesson. One I barely survived, to be sure, after my tumble down the stair, but one I am glad I learned. If a gentleman does not say he loves you, you must listen. You must listen to what is said, and what is not said. We cannot force others to feel for us. Falling in love with a man who did not love me broke my heart, and it broke my pride." It also broke her hip, Georgette thought with a rather wry smile. "However, now I know to not risk myself for someone who does not love me. I know that it is never worth playing the fool for a man who does not care."

The Duke nodded. "I feel I ought to apologize, for the behavior of my friend and my sister."

"Why? You are not accountable for their actions," she said.

"You are correct, and yet, as they are unlikely to ever apologize to you, I must stand in. My sister Judith has long been spoilt, and my friend does not possess the character to counter it."

She shrugged. She did not wish to speak of Lady Judith and Sebastien.

"It was a long time ago. I am much changed now."

He grinned. "Yes, now you steal notes from potted plants, break cryptic cyphers and play Beethoven."

He sighed and looked at the clock on the mantelpiece.

"I must go," he said. "But I will see you tomorrow, for the ball."

"Yes. Fanny is looking forward to it."

"And you?" The Duke asked. "Are you looking forward to it?"

"I am," she said softly, and realized she meant it. She was looking forward to seeing him again.

Part 3

A Visit to Vauxhall

12

he Duke of Eversley entered Hampstead Heath in the early morning light. He had received a note from Mr. White when he returned home the previous day, after searching Meryton's apartments and visiting Miss Quinby. The note informed him that Mr. White wished to meet him on the Heath the next morning.

The morning frost had not yet disappeared, and the leaves and stalks glittered and sparkled in the winter sun. His horse picked his way along the path

He loved the Heath. Unlike the other parks, and even the estates in the country favored by many of the nobles, the Heath had retained its wildness. Blanche had always loved the Heath as well; she even loved the ever-present possibility that they might be accosted by highwaymen and footpads.

He could see her now, as if she were riding alongside him. She'd had a delicate little brown mare named Marie.

Dressed in her royal blue riding habit, that matched her beautiful blue eyes, a jaunty little hat atop the pile of blond hair, she would gallop about the Heath, laughing at the birds that would startle and fly up. Then she would trot up alongside him, her breath visible in the winter cold.

"Charles," she would say. "Do you not wish to race?"

And he would say something gallant, about how he could not possibly race ahead of her, for then he would not be able to see her or admire her, doing something she loved to do. And she would laugh, and dash off once more, never able to stay by his side for too long.

But she did not gallop anymore, he thought as he watched her ghost disappear over a crest and Mr. White appear in her place. She was dead, killed by the rabble in France.

Mr. White was walking, and so Eversley swung himself off his horse and slowly walked towards the man.

"Eversley," White said.

He nodded. "You sent word you wished to see me?"

White sniffed and drew out a handkerchief. "Beg your pardon," he said as he wiped his nose. "I seem to have a bit of a cold."

It was odd, thinking that Mr. White was subject to the same vicissitudes of life as everyone else, Eversley thought. He'd always imagined White lead a life untouched by maladies especially something as mundane as a cold.

"How goes it with Meryton?" White asked.

"He's a terrible gambler who is in love with an heiress and held back by a misguided sense of pride," Eversley said. "But he isn't Lightfoot. I imagine you knew this, even when you assigned me to track him."

Mr. White blinked.

"If Lightfoot has a list of spies, he knows me to be one," Eversley said. "You would not be so foolish as to assign someone the man knows to be a spy to follow him. You would only assign someone who you know to not be on the list. I cannot help but believe I am merely a decoy; an attempt to lead the real Lightfoot to believe that we are fooled, that we would seriously consider Merry Meryton to be a traitor."

White looked at him. Then he let out a small laugh. "I was hoping you would not make such a deduction."

"And I was embarrassed the deduction took me so long to make," Eversley said.

"I must tell you, we need you to continue to pretend you consider Meryton a threat; to continue to follow him."

Eversley shrugged. "It's no difficulty for me," he said. "I like Merry. I wish he would stop trying to win his fortune by gambling, but we cannot control the lives of others, as much as we might wish to."

White gave him a quizzical look. "If anyone can, it would be you," he said. "You are a duke, after all. Nevertheless, I appreciate that you refrain from being excessively dictatorial."

"Perhaps I shall take it up," Eversley said. "I begin to suspect my days of espionage may be coming to an end. No doubt I will need to find a way to spend my time."

White nodded. "I imagine the Duke of Eversley has many affairs to which he might devote himself. Perhaps you might give some additional attention to parliament. Or to your estates."

It was a mild rebuke, but Eversley felt it nonetheless. He had been grieving, damn it. And he had served his country. The last decade had not been in vain.

Still, it echoed the sentiments that had been rattling inside his own brain. Why was he creeping around gaming halls and darkened streets and heaths, when there was even more he could be doing?

He shook such thoughts away. "How long do you need me to continue to follow Meryton?" he asked.

Mr. White coughed. "Unfortunately, I cannot say," he said. "We believe the list has not yet been passed to the French. Our sources suggest that they are still gathering the funds that have been demanded."

"Do you know who the true Lightfoot is?" Eversley asked.

"We believe we do," Mr. White said. "However, we have no conclusive proof."

Eversley's horse nudged him, and he rubbed the equine's muzzle and scratched in the groove under his chin. When he stopped, the horse nudged him again, very much like a dog insisting upon attention. "Very well," he said to White as he gave the animal a final pat. "I shall continue to tail Merry. I do hope you manage to thwart the man before the list is passed along."

Mr. White laughed again. "So do I, Eversley," he said. "So do I."

He nodded to the Duke and then turned, to go back the way he came, giving a brief wave as he disappeared.

Eversley stared after him. He wondered what White

did, when he was not directing a variety of men and women regarding clandestine affairs. He liked to think that the man returned home to a warm and friendly wife, the type that gathered in crying children and let them dry their tears on her shoulder, and delicious hot food and good ale. Maybe she was just a little plump, with an ample bosom to hold the old man close. He hoped he was right.

He stared back over the Heath. The sun was fully up, the frost nearly melted. He wondered what Miss Quinby was doing. Perhaps she was having breakfast. Or playing her piano. Perhaps she was still abed, her cheeks rosy from sleeping near the fire.

What was he doing? Thinking of Miss Quinby, sleeping? He shook himself. This association was turning into more than mere friendship. It had been madness, slipping into her home yesterday, dressed as a manservant. If the *Ton* ever gathered such gossip, her reputation would be well and truly ruined. And yet, he had needed to see her, to speak with her, and she had not seemed to mind his unorthodox entry.

This was more than friendship, but it could not continue. He could not become attached. He would not. He could not betray Blanche.

GEORGETTE and her cousin Fanny had elected to go shopping that morning, and were making their way through the shops on Bond Street.

"What shall you wear to the ball this evening?" Fanny

asked. Fanny was hoping to find some elegant lace gloves that might match the lace bodice of her ball gown. Georgette, on the other hand, had been hoping to locate a nice comb that she might wear in her hair for the ball.

"Mmmm," she muttered noncommittally as she perused the offerings on display. "I'm not entirely certain what I shall wear. No doubt whatever I may wear, you shall put me quite in the shade. You always look so lovely in a ball gown, and your lace is exquisite. Is this a good match?" She asked picking up a pair of gloves.

Fanny gave her a dry look. "You haven't settled then?" she asked. "You have not given it any thought?" She took the gloves and tried them on. They were a perfect fit.

Georgette blinked back innocently.

"Liar," Fanny said. "I've no doubt you've agonized over what to wear for hours. It is quite possible the Duke will ask you to stand up with him, you know. You must look very fine. I will take these," Fanny said to the hovering shop girl. "I will wrap them up right away," the girl said.

"I believe the Duke was injured last year," Georgette told Fanny. "Dancing is somewhat uncomfortable for him. And you know very well that hopping about aggravates my hip."

Fanny stuck out her lower lip. "Not even one dance?"

"It is the burden I must bear for once being a young, headstrong, overly passionate woman," Georgette said, with a wink.

"You list these traits as if they are undesirable."

"Not on you, dear cousin." Georgette patted Fanny's arm. "Never on you."

How odd, she mused. When did it stop mattering

quite so much, what happened to her years ago? When did she stop thinking of Sebastien and her fall down the stair as quite so tragic? The only tragedy she currently felt was that she could not dance with Eversley. She would have liked to dance with him. To join hands, to smell the scent of him as she was held in his arms however briefly. She had always enjoyed dancing. It was a shame she had to content herself with tapping her toes on the sideline.

"Mr. Rupert Fellows will also accompany us to the ball," Fanny said to her, as they left one of the arcades and exited onto Oxford Street. "He offered, and I thought that might allow the Duke to focus solely on you for the evening."

Georgette laughed. "Fanny, you must not set your heart on this. I have told you. The Duke and I are merely friends. And barely that, if I am entirely honest. You mustn't hope for something that shall not be."

"Very well," Fanny said. "Because he is chaperoning us merely in the position as your friend, the Duke may focus entirely on you this evening. The two of you, unable to dance, may sit on the edge of the room and attract the side-line glances of the *Ton*, while Mr. Rupert Fellows and I dance a shocking three dances together; thereby solidifying my reputation as a fast young lady who will never come to any good."

"As your chaperon, I absolutely forbid it. If you are going to shock the *Ton*, you must dance at the very least five dances with the young gentlemen. Three is so very un-extraordinary."

"You say this, but you aren't the one who must make

the sacrifice of dancing with him. Have you seen Fellows dance? Goodness, it's like dancing with a small child, only a quite heavy child. He trod on my feet at least four times when we last danced."

"Why in heaven's name then, would you be contemplating three dances?" Georgette asked. She gave her charge a small frown.

"It is quite amusing to be sure, and he certainly enjoys himself dancing, but it is exhausting nonetheless," Fanny said.

"Oh? Well then, perhaps, rather than risk your reputation and your feet, you should only dance two dances with the young man," Georgette said slyly thinking perhaps her cousin had taken a liking to Mr. Fellows despite his lackluster dancing talents.

"It will not matter how many dances I dance. No one will be watching me. Everyone will be watching you and the Duke." Fanny deflected.

"I should have left you to survive a season with Aunt Agatha," Georgette said, swatting at her cousin.

"Don't say that. Not even in jest. Future duchesses should never threaten anyone with Aunt Agatha." Fanny laughed then, a gay and tinkling laugh, and danced away, out of Georgette's reach. "Come," she said. "I want to have plenty of time to try new hair styles."

"What were you thinking?" Georgette asked.

"Not for me. For you," Fanny corrected as she waved an airy hand and headed for the door.

Georgette watched her young cousin with a mixture of love and aggravation. She owed much to Fanny. No other cousin had stood so steadfastly by her over the years. No other cousin had insisted she return to Town, to assume chaperone duties. Without Fanny, she would have continued to wallow in the country, possibly forever.

It was easy to wallow, she thought. She had been perfectly content to accept that her life would never be especially grand. That was her penance; that was her punishment for the extraordinary passion she had displayed in her youth. She would spend the rest of her days at the manor, occasionally walking into the village. She would visit Mrs. Darby, with her troubled foot, and Mrs. Butterworth, with her troubled daughter. She would visit Mr. Kempton, her father's old steward, and Mrs. Pritchard, her old nurse. She would take biscuits and preserves to the tenants, and exchange books of Latin with Mr. Moresby and notes in code with the curate.

It was a good life, she thought. She had risen up and made herself a good life. She had no complaints.

And yet, it had been ever so slightly dull...ever so slightly devoid of emotion. She enjoyed the visits and the notes and the Latin and the walks to the village, but none of it had excited her as much as the promise of an evening escorted by the Duke of Eversley did. None of it brought color to her cheeks or a twinge to her stomach.

Tonight, she thought. Tonight, she would see him again. She lay a hand on her stomach. She could barely contain the butterflies.

13

*E*versley trotted his horse into the courtyard of his mansion. He dismounted and handed the reins to the waiting stable boy.

The door opened before he reached the top step. His butler, Rokesby, stood aside and held the door open.

"Breakfast is served in the breakfast room, Your Grace, if you wish it."

Eversley rubbed his hands together. "Certainly," he said. "I could do with a spot of coffee as well, if you think Mrs. Swinton could rustle some up. I was thinking of coffee just now."

Rokesby's face remained as calm as ever. "Yes, Your Grace, we shall see to it that you have a pot straight away."

Eversley was tempted to apologize. During his time in France, he had made do with very few servants. Yes, Mr. Murphy and James and Joseph had accompanied his throughout, ostensibly in the roles of drivers and footmen and all around manservants. But in reality they operated less as servants and more as accomplices and aides for his more clandestine activities. They certainly did not often have time to fix him a pot of coffee. He had fallen out of the habit of ordering and expecting immediate service.

He had the sense that Rokesby greatly disapproved of this decline. Perhaps he thought his job was in jeopardy if the Duke became too independent. Eversley could have told him that was not the case.

Eversley made his way to the breakfast room, where dishes of hot food were set out.

"Such excess," Blanche would always say. "There are but two of us. We cannot eat so much." Strangely enough, her marriage and life apart from the French court seemed to make her so much more aware of the shortcomings of the French aristocrats although her own parents were not in line for the Crown. They had no special interests in government. There was no reason to kill them, or Blanche.

"Surely they will be safe from the storm," she had said, and he had agreed with her.

"They are only a few disgruntled peasants," he had said, "How much harm can they cause?" How much indeed. He had been so wrong.

He blinked back to the present, and looked at the mounds of food. "I trust the extra is passed along to the servants afterwards," he said, as he always did.

"Mrs. Swinton would never allow it to go to waste," the butler assured him.

"Good. Good."

The next line in this parody, he remembered was Blanche announcing she would speak to the housekeeper personally, and the housekeeper assuring Blanche that the servants would enjoy the remainder of any of the food. It had become their routine, played out again and again. Why had the rabble not known that Blanche would have shared her last morsel with them? They had condemned her simply because she was rich, just as so many rich condemned the poor as lazy simply because they were poor. When had the world gone so mad?

As he fixed his plate, he waited to hear Blanche's voice, to feel her presence drift into the room. She often came when he sat alone at table, but today, there was nothing but silence, the sounds of his cutlery on the china, the tiny creak of a floorboard as a footman shifted position.

She did not always appear at breakfast. He knew this. Sometimes, if he was preoccupied by other thoughts, if he was involved in a particularly difficult assignment, he would keep her at bay. But this morning? He expected her. He needed her.

Where was she? She had galloped off at the Heath, and not returned. He wanted to tell her that his suspicions regarding Mr. White's request that he follow Merry had been confirmed. He wanted to tell her that Merry had never really been suspected of betraying the Crown. The thought loosened the tightness in his throat. He had not seriously believed Merry a traitor. And she would say, "*Mais oui,* I could have told you that, *mon Chéri.*"

Just like Miss Quinby. He had told her first. He had

not even thought to tell Blanche yesterday. He had wanted to tell Miss Quinby, and so he had.

He set down his fork and knife. Perhaps she was somewhere else, in another room of the house. He would find her. He stood and made to leave the room.

"Your coffee, my Grace?" A footman had just entered via the servants' door, holding a pot of fresh coffee.

Eversley looked at him blankly. "No," he finally managed to say. "I find I no longer desire it. Excuse me."

He made his way up to the bedroom. Sometimes, in the mornings, if he went for an early ride without her, she would wait for him in bed with a pot of chocolate. Perhaps she would be there, nestled in among the pillows, the bed curtains pulled aside.

But the room was empty. Dust motes drifted through the sunlight that streamed in through the windows. The room had been recently cleaned, he could tell. The grate had been scrubbed and a fire set.

He rubbed his jaw. He should shave.

Perhaps she would be in one of the sitting rooms. She enjoyed the south-facing one in winter, as it let in the best light. She would sit in front of the window and read her novels, sometimes English ones, and other times scandalous French ones. He remembered reading those ones together, giggling like school children and kissing. Would Miss Quinby read novels with him, he wondered. The thought of Miss Quinby filled his mind, wisteria perfume changing to strawberries. He made his way back down to the first floor, to the sitting room.

A maid, busy polishing the furniture looked up.

"Oh! Begging your pardon, Your Grace," she said. She bobbed a curtsy and quickly gathered her rags and polish. She began to leave the room.

He waved her to stillness. "No, no," he said. "I did not mean to disturb you. Carry on."

Perhaps the drawing room then. But when he strode into the middle of the room, she was not there. There was no hint of her, no scent, neither wisteria, nor strawberry.

The nursery? Eversley made his way up the stairs to that long abandoned room. The furniture was draped with dust covers. It had never been used; at least not by them. For a moment the grief almost overwhelmed him. They had been hoping, before she left for France, for a child.

"Yes, but I worry," Blanche had teased. "What if our child is like you? I have no doubt you a little tyrant when you were young."

"I was not," he had retorted. "I was a perfect angel."

Blanche had snorted at this remark and gave him a long suffering look. "What happened?" she teased, and he had kissed her.

Then she had left for France, promising to be back soon, and he never saw her again.

She was not here, among this sad furniture draped in sheets. She was not in the music room. Why would she be? She disliked playing. The pure notes of Beethoven sounded in his imagination and continued to play as he walked. She was not in the library, or his office, but the music continued.

He was riffling through the clutter in the attic store

room, searching for her, even though, he knew full well, she was not here. She was dead. All of the music went silent. He was still musing when his butler interrupted him.

"I beg your pardon, Your Grace," he said. "Were you still planning on escorting Miss Quinby and her cousin to the ball? Would you like if we drew you a bath, so that you might begin to prepare?"

A ball? A bath? He looked up. The attic was darker than it had been; Rokesby stood mostly in shadow.

"What time is it?" he asked his butler.

"It is early evening, Your Grace. You may wish to depart in a couple of hours."

A couple of hours? Where had the day gone? He looked around. Crates and trunks had been pried open, possessions scattered everywhere.

She wasn't here. He knew it. He knew why. And what he had to do.

"Rokesby, please forgive me. I was searching for something, but appear to have misplaced it. Kindly have someone tidy this up."

Rokesby nodded.

Eversley made his way to the stairs. "I do not believe I will be able to escort the ladies after all. I will pen a note of regret right away. If we might deliver it to them as quickly as possible? I must attend to other matters."

For a moment, something flickered across the butler's face. Was it censure? Just as quickly as it crossed his face, it was gone. His face returned to its normally placid state.

"Certainly, Your Grace."

GEORGETTE SAT STILL as her maid carefully fixed her hair. She was wearing a gorgeous gown, of light blue silk gauze over satin. She could see herself in the mirror, in the glow of candlelight. She looked rather well.

Fanny sat at the other dressing table. They had developed the habit of readying themselves for balls together in the same room. It allowed for them to chatter and converse with each other and their maids.

There was a knock at the door. Another maid entered, bearing a silver salver. A note sat atop.

"This was just delivered, Miss," she said, presenting the note to Georgette.

"Oh? I wonder what it might be." Georgette smiled at her maid, who stepped back from her hair. She reached for the note.

"What a fine seal," she said.

She stopped and looked at it more closely. It was the Duke's seal, hastily stamped into fine red wax. Carefully, she broke it open.

She read the lines once, then twice, then a third time. Each time they were the same.

Georgette swallowed. She blinked carefully and took deep breaths. It should not signify.

"Well?" Fanny asked. "Whatever is it?"

"The Duke..." Georgette cleared the catch in her throat. "sends his regrets. He is unable to accompany us tonight."

"What?" Fanny looked as baffled as Georgette felt. She gave a small laugh. "Surely you must be jesting."

Georgette shook her head slowly and held the note out to Fanny, who took it. Fanny's eyes ran back and forth from left to right as she skimmed the note. Her brow puckered, a tiny dent forming in the middle, as she digested the contents. She looked up at Georgette.

"He sends his regrets," she said.

Georgette nodded.

Fanny looked at her searchingly. Georgette attempted to smooth away any pain from her face. She did not wish her cousin to know she was feeling quite so affected. She smiled.

"You mustn't take it to heart, Fanny," she said. "His is a Duke. No doubt he has any number of important obligations."

Indeed, Georgette knew this to be true. The man was a spy, for God's sake. He most certainly had important obligations. Why, as they spoke, he could very possibly be apprehending the mysterious Englishman. Or mistakenly pursuing another man like Merry. She would not know.

But she could not help feeling that perhaps this was more. Was he truly taken away by another obligation? Or did he simply not wish to see her? What if he had realized her feelings for him were growing? Could he perhaps have sensed her joy at seeing him yesterday, her eager anticipation over seeing him today?

No doubt that was it, she thought. She should not have been so transparently pleased to see him. She should have remained somewhat detached. And yet, she had been so overjoyed to meet a man with whom she could be herself.

"Sends. His. Regrets." Fanny was enunciating each

word, her voice rising as she did. "Sends his regrets? Well you know what I have to say to that, Georgette? I say, stuff his regrets. I do not give a fig if he is a Duke. I shall never forgive him for slighting you in such a manner. Sends his regrets. I do not believe it."

Fanny's outrage was so pure; it was comforting, and almost amusing. Georgette forced herself to adopt a lighter tone.

"Fanny, my dear," she laughed. "Really. I am fine. It is of no importance. And your Mr. Rupert Fellows will still be here to accompany us to the ball."

"Yes, Rupert." Fanny ran a hand through her hair absently. The maid standing behind her gave a tiny moan and started forward, then remembered her place and clasped her hands together, despite very clearly wishing to fix the stray bits of Fanny's hair that were now standing up.

"I have it," Fanny said, suddenly.

Georgette looked up. Her cousin's eyes were alight. "Oh, no," Georgette said. She shook her head. "I know this look. Whenever you get this look, I wind up in Astley's Ampitheatre, nearly set on fire."

"That was but the one time," Fanny said. "And I apologized profusely. But we shall not go to the ball tonight."

"No?" Georgette asked. That actually might be nice. She could change into her nightgown and settle in for the evening with a novel. And maybe a small glass of sherry.

"We shall go to Vauxhall."

"Vauxhall?" Georgette's dreams of a quiet night at home disappeared.

"Yes, Vauxhall. There are balls every evening. And they are all the same. I don't see why we should go to a ball and listen to everyone around us gossip in tones that are just audible enough to hear. I have no desire to be crushed amongst packs of sweaty unwashed bodies and forced to drink ratafia. No, we shall go to Vauxhall."

"You realize there are packs of sweaty unwashed bodies there, do you not?" Georgette asked.

"Certainly, but at least it is outside, and it is cold enough most of the scent will be contained by coats and wraps and blown away on the wind. Furthermore, I have a strong desire for thinly sliced ham and a waterfall display."

Georgette blew out a breath. Vauxhall. She had not been there since she was engaged to Sebastien. Perhaps it would be good for her; a distracting amusement, with no dukes to turn her stomach into knots.

"Very well," she said. She smiled at Fanny. "Let us go to Vauxhall instead." She looked down at her gown, and then up at Sarah. "I fear I shall have to change to something more substantial," she said to the maid.

Sarah nodded. "Certainly, miss."

Fanny grinned. "Excellent," she said. "Delia Ditherfield is meant to be there tonight, with Mr. Foster. We can join their party."

"Mr. Foster? Has she given up on Meryton, then?"

"Never. But her father is determined to distract her," Fanny said.

"Would he allow her to marry Merry, if the gentleman ever asks?"

"To be sure, he would. I do believe he is so tired of

listening to Delia howl over the supper table, he would do anything. But Meryton has not offered."

The two of them stared at each other for a moment, clearly thing the same thing.

"Men," they both said at the same time, shaking their heads in dismay.

14

*E*versley stared down at the cards that sat upon the green baize. Here he was, again, back at the club, back at the table, next to Merry. The cards blurred in front of him. How were there two of the same queen?

He had had too much to drink.

Merry was once again raising the stakes beyond his means and mopping his brow. Eversley hoped that Lightfoot was somewhere in this room, watching him dogging steps, because otherwise he was going to toss himself off the roof.

Goodness, he was turning into Miss Quinby. He grinned to himself. She would enjoy the irony. She would tell him to mind the stair.

He should not be thinking of Miss Quinby. He shook his head. It felt as if he had a pouch of coins in between his ears, shifting from right to left. He did not want to think of Miss Quinby. He wanted to think of Blanche.

He had sworn. After Blanche, he had sworn. Never again.

He looked back at the cards. Somehow they had changed. Had he placed a bet? He placed a hand on Merry's shoulder.

"I do believe I've had too much to drink, my dear fellow. The cards are positively swimming."

Merry nodded slowly. "They do every evening," he whispered, confidingly, to Eversley. "Every evening the cards begin to swim."

"Why?" Eversley asked.

"I really cannot say," Merry said, nodding. "I imagine it's to do with the drink."

"No," Eversley said, more forcefully this time. "No. Why every night?"

"You've lost me," Merry said.

"Why are we here?" Eversley asked. He shook his head again. "Oh, bother. I know why I am here. Why are you here, Merry?"

"I must win my fortune," Merry said, easily. He shrugged. "It is the only way."

"No," Eversley said. "No, it is not the only way. You could simply propose to Miss Ditherfield. You do not have to be here."

"I explained it all before," Merry said. "I cannot approach her empty-handed."

"You run the risk of never approaching her at all," Eversley said. Why did Merry insist on being so blind? Would he forever sit at these tables, refusing to sacrifice his pride? Would he never understand how precious these moments might be?

"I love her," Merry said. "I told you. I cannot approach her, unable to provide for her."

"She can provide for herself," Eversley said. "She's a bloody heiress, after all."

"Be careful how you speak of her," Merry said. "I will not hear anyone besmirch her name in my presence."

"I'm not besmirching it, you fool. I'm simply baffled as to why you refuse yourself happiness."

The play at the table had suspended. The other gentlemen, uninterested in affairs of the heart, and disinclined to witness an intense conversation between two drunk men, slowly drifted off to other tables.

"I refuse myself happiness?" Merry asked, his voice incredulous. "This, from the man who shunned society for nigh on a decade, after his wife died. Who now trots around after me, gambling when he does not require the funds, drinking when he does not require the drink. What of you, Your Grace?"

"What of me?" Eversley demanded.

"When will you accept Her Grace's death?" Merry asked. "I thought you had finally returned, the man whom I considered a friend throughout school and university, that you had finally come to peace. Do you have any idea how difficult it has been for so many of us, to watch you fall into despair?"

Eversley blinked. What? How long had Merry Meryton been observing him?

"I..." he started. "You've been discussing me?"

Merry snorted. "Not at all Eversley. You're merely a duke, one of the wealthiest and most powerful figures in the land, who has disappeared for the last ten years, after the death of his French wife, to mourn and lament her. No, we have not discussed you at all."

Eversley looked about. There were men all over this club, men he had considered friends or, if not friends, close acquaintances. Men he'd been at school with, men who owned land near his, men in Parliament, men belonging to his many clubs. They had all been aware of his grief.

And here, he had just been following Merry. He wanted to laugh. No doubt they assumed he was gambling away his life as well. He had become a tragic figure. It was a good thing he had not voiced his thought to fling himself off the roof, out loud.

"Merry," he said. "You needn't worry about me."

Merry snorted.

"No, I tell you," Eversley said. "You need not worry about me. You should be worrying about yourself. Your feelings for Miss Ditherfield, your pursuit for ready funds. Merry, this cannot continue."

Merry puffed up, much like the peacocks that ran about one of Eversley's estates, brought there by an earlier inhabitant. Then he deflated.

"I love her," he said. "I love her, and I wish to be with her. But I do not know how I can come to her as I am."

Eversley sighed. There would be no solutions tonight. Merry refused to propose unless he had more to offer. The Duke knew enough to know that the only person who could persuade Merry would be Merry himself.

"All I ask is that you consider what it is to lose the woman you love," Eversley said to his friend. "I lost mine to a horde of people. If Miss Ditherfield accepts the proposal of another, the only one you will have to blame will be yourself."

Merry opened his mouth to say something more. Then his gaze shifted to the person behind Eversley.

"Fletcher," Merry said, stiffly. "Fancy seeing you here."

Eversley stifled a groan. He did not want to speak with Lord Fletcher. Not now. Nevertheless, he fixed a pleasant look on his face and turned.

"Fletcher," he said, attempting a smile. "How goes it?"

Fletcher nodded, his fleshy jowls wobbling, his beady eyes looking between the two of them. He settled down into one of the empty seats at the table.

"Must say, I don't remember the two of you being so close before," he said.

"Before?" Eversley asked, coolly.

"Yes, before your wife died," Fletcher said. "I did not realize you and Meryton were such close friends."

Eversley shrugged. "Times change."

"Oh, I say, are we starting a game?" Lord Brockton settled down into the empty chair. He rubbed his hands, looking at the three gentlemen at the table. "This will be good," he said.

Merry's eyes once more filled with anticipation. He nodded at Brockton's invitation for a game.

Eversley sighed. He signaled for another drink.

15

Georgette had to admit that Mr. Rupert Fellows had exhibited surprising depths of resourcefulness this evening. The gentleman, whom she had always considered to be a bit of a rattle, had barely so much as blinked when Fanny informed him they would no longer be attending the ball. He had also managed to produce a boat at Westminster, and quite easily ferried them across the Thames to the Gardens.

The weather was cold, but not freezing, and many people were making their way across to the gardens. The Thames was alight with the glimmering lanterns of ferries and barges.

Eventually they docked, and Mr. Fellows assisted the ladies as they alighted. Then Vauxhall was before them.

Georgette had always adored Vauxhall. As a young lady, she had fancied it to be a magical place, fitting for her mood; so in love with Sebastien, the lanterns and waterfall, the fireworks, people from all walks of life. Even the exorbitantly-priced and thinly-sliced ham. She loved it all.

She remembered Sebastien laughing at her when she had told him she even loved the ham. "This does not surprise me," he had said. "Ladies who have never had to consider the price of food enjoy thin slices of ham. I have observed this behavior more than once."

She should have known so much sooner, she thought now, that Sebastien was only interested in her money and in fact appeared to possess a good amount of disrespect for her. Poor Sebastien. She hoped he was happy with an even greater heiress.

It was a good reminder for her, however. She needed to remember to not become attached to another gentleman. Only grief and lost pride could result. Today was a good example. For a moment, she had allowed herself to feel for the Duke. No doubt he had realized her affection. She imagined he had been quite disgusted with her for it. How could she disregard his wife, the one, true love of his life, and feel for her? How could she believe that the friend of her erstwhile fiancé would be interested in her?

Her cheeks burned with mortification, fortunate for her that the gardens were already dark.

"There is Delia!" Fanny pointed a gloved finger towards her friend, who was in another party alighting from a boat. "How fortunate!"

She called after Delia and dragged Georgette over to the Ditherfield party.

Delia clapped as she saw the two ladies arrive. "I did

not know you would be here," she said. "I would have invited you to join our party."

"You may invite us now," Fanny told her. "I promise Mr. Fellows shall not mind."

"Mr. Fellows?" Delia blinked. "I had believed the Duke intended to escort you tonight."

"Yes, well." Fanny looked slightly put out by her friend's memory. "He sent his regrets."

Delia looked at Georgette in surprise. Georgette nodded, confirming.

"I do not believe it," Delia said. "Perhaps we should form a club," she said to Georgette. "Ladies in love with stupid men."

Georgette opened her mouth to tell Delia that she was she was not in love with the Duke. They were merely friends, and after his regrets this evening, not even especially good friends. Then she realized that she was his friend, no matter.

Georgette was still standing there, her mouth half open to correct Delia, when Mr. Foster appeared.

"And who might these lovely ladies be?" he asked.

Delia introduced Georgette and Fanny, as her particular friends, to Mr. Foster, who was all that was amiable. He was wealthy and had a vast estate in Hertfordshire, and his manners were excellent. He spoke with a quiet precision as if every word must be weighed.

Georgette could see why Delia could not stand him. The others of the party had now crowded around them, and were asking which direction they should take.

"I'm afraid it appears all of the supper boxes have

been engaged," Mr. Foster announced. "But no matter, we shall survive."

Mr. Rupert Fellows joined them at that moment. "You shall simply have to join us," he told the others. "I have managed to procure a box for Miss Markham and Miss Quinby and myself. There is certainly room to spare."

The entire party looked at him. Georgette wondered if this truly was the same man who had trod on Fanny's feet several times the last time they danced.

Fanny evidently felt likewise. "Why Fellows," she declared, "you astonish me."

He gave Fanny his arm and positively beamed.

THEY MADE their way down the Grand Walk. The lanterns had been lit, and the gardens were truly magnificent. Around them, other people strutted, taking in the sights; families, lovers, and dangerous young men looking to lure away unaccompanied females.

They could hear the orchestra playing. Georgette thrilled at the idea of music. She nestled in her fur-lined cloak. She was glad of its warmth. It was still cold, despite all of the lights and thrills around them.

Delia took her arm. "Walk with me," she told Georgette. "If I am seen with another lady, Mr. Foster will not press upon me quite so much."

"Certainly," Georgette said. They walked in silence for a few moments, enjoying the sights. "Is he so very bad? Foster?"

Delia sighed. "No," she said. "But he is not Mr.

Meryton." She shrugged. "Nevertheless, I begin to wonder if perhaps I must let Merry go." She took a deep breath and exhaled. "But tonight, I refuse to think about such matters. Rather than think of Merry, I shall be merry!"

Georgette laughed. "Very clever," she said.

The group continued along their way, passing by acrobats and other entertainers.

Two men, cloaked in black, passed Georgette and Delia, headed in the opposite direction.

"Oui, je lui ai dit," one of them said.

Georgette stopped. It was him! The Frenchman from the British Museum. She twisted, to watch the men.

"Delia, come with me," she whispered. Delia, whose eyes had widened when Georgette had stopped so abruptly, gamely nodded. Georgette turned them and followed the men.

They were speaking French. Blast! She had never bothered much with French. She'd been more distracted by mathematics and reading and music.

"Is there any chance you speak French?" she asked Delia quietly.

Delia nodded. "I learned at school," she said. "It was my best subject."

"Grand," Georgette said. "Can you hear what those men are saying?"

Delia nodded again.

"Good," Georgette said. "Remember what they say. We must keep following them, but cannot let them see us."

Delia licked her lips. "Excellent," she said. "I love an adventure."

The two followed the men, who turned off onto one

of the dark paths. Georgette could make out phrases and bits, but had no idea what they were saying. She hoped Delia was paying close attention.

Eventually, the men stopped along the path. It became clear that they would be separating: they stood in with the postures of an imminent goodbye. Georgette looked around. It appeared the one of them, a man she had not recognized, would take the path to the right, back towards the orchestra. The other could either continue forward, or turn back.

"Don't turn back," she whispered, under her breath.

He turned back. He paused when he saw the ladies, standing so near.

"Keep walking," Georgette muttered to Delia under her breath. "Pretend we are simply ladies exploring the gardens."

"Only naughty ladies explore the gardens," Delia said.

"I suppose that makes us naughty ladies," Georgette said.

"Excellent. I shall tell Mr. Meryton and drive him into a rage."

They sauntered forward, as if there was nothing odd about encountering two lone men in this darkened path. And it appeared as if he intended to let them glide by. Georgette began to give a sigh of relief.

His hand shot out. His fingers curled around her arm.

"Well, well, well," he said. "What have we here?"

His French accent was thick. It was just as she remembered standing near the Rosetta Stone.

"Unhand me, sir," she said, attempting to sound steady.

"And why should I wish to do that?" He laughed, a mocking laugh. "Here I find two ladies. *Les deux poulettes.* Why should I not stop to play?"

His tone was sinister and threatening. Georgette's stomach clenched.

"There you are!"

They all turned. Mr. Rupert Fellows was ambling down the path. He bore more than passing resemblance to a Labrador, Georgette thought. He grinned happily.

"Fanny is terribly put out with you two," he said. He looked eagerly at the two of them. "She had every intention of toeing the line of respectability and exploring the dark paths herself. And then the two of you left her with the rest of the party. She is positively seething, I will have you know. I had to promise her I would find you both and restore you back to the supper box, safe and sound."

He gave the Frenchman a friendly slap on the back. The man let out what sounded like a groan. Then Mr. Fellows took his hand. "My thanks," he said to the man. "For seeing these ladies went unharmed. Capitol, capital."

Bowing, he took the hands of the two ladies and tucked them into the crook of his arm and led them away.

Georgette cocked her head and stared at him as they walked.

"Mr. Fellows, how in heaven's name did you find us?" she asked.

He grinned. "I've five younger sisters," he said.

"Say no more," Georgette said. She laughed. She had been about to ask the man if he too was a secret spy. But no. No, he was not. He was an older brother.

He restored them to the supper box, where Fanny was deliberately ignoring them. Georgette, recognizing her cousin's hurt. Fanny could never bear to be left out, and it looked as though Georgette had purposely left her, to say nothing of the fact that she was not exactly an attentive chaperone. Georgette sat next to Fanny and patted her arm.

"I'm terribly sorry I dragged Delia away," she said. "But I needed someone who understood French."

Fanny's brow lifted. "French?" she asked. Her mouth set. "I understand French."

"Your French tutor swore to never teach again after having you," Georgette said. "I meant, I needed someone who understood French, not simply parroted French phrases—badly."

She knew Fanny wished to refute her, but it was true. She bit her lip.

"Tell me a single phrase you remember in French," Georgette challenged.

"Not in polite company," Fanny said.

Georgette laughed.

The curses words the family had learned when Fanny's tutor finally turned in his resignation had been truly remarkable. Georgette still heard Fanny use them under her breath when she was truly upset.

Fanny gave a huff of exasperation. "Why did you need someone who understood French?" she asked.

"I cannot explain all of it," Georgette said. "It isn't my secret to share. But I believe that the man we followed is engaged is some very nefarious dealings. I overheard him some days ago, when we were at the British Museum."

She turned to Delia. "Can you tell me what you heard?"

Delia nodded and leaned forward eagerly. "The two men were discussing how to transport money. They were saying that they had the necessary coin. Then one of them said that he would be contacting the man about the exchange. I could not quite tell who this man was. They simply referred to him as the Englishman."

Georgette nodded. It was the same Frenchman! And they had been discussing the very same transaction she had overheard at the British Museum! What were the chances? They had to be extremely low. If she were a betting woman, she would have bet against the odds.

It was Fate, she thought. She'd long suspected that Fate had played a heavy hand with her. Tripping her down the stair rather than allowing her to toss herself off the roof. Leading her out into the garden, where the Duke had been smoking a cigar. Sitting her next to the potted plant, where the cryptic note had been left. But this last one, it truly defied belief. Had the Duke not sent his regrets, Fanny would not have been disgruntled enough to insist on Vauxhall. And if they had not arrived when they did, if Delia had not taken her arm, if Mr. Rupert Fellows had demonstrated heretofore unplumbed depths, she would never have heard or seen the Frenchman again.

Please, Fate, she thought. Please give me just a tiny bit more.

"Did they say anything else?" she asked Delia. "Any details about the exchange?"

Delia chewed her lip, thinking. "They said a man

would bring it to the ball, but neither said which ball. They only said he would meet them in the Rose Room."

"The Rose Room?" Fanny groaned. "Why? Why is there always a Rose Room. No doubt it is yellow and covered with Egyptian artifacts."

Georgette smiled. But then she thought more about what Delia said. "Were there no other details?" she asked.

Delia chewed her lip once more. Then shook her head. "That was all," she said.

Georgette rubbed her forehead. So close!

"I believe Delia and I might need a bit more explanation," Fanny said.

Could she tell them? She did not wish to betray The Duke's confidences. And yet, if they wanted to stop the Frenchman, she would need Fanny and Delia's help. Perhaps she could reveal a small amount.

"It is my understanding that a certain Englishman managed to take a very valuable document. I don't know precisely what was contained in this document, but I do believe it is vital in our war efforts against France."

Fanny and Delia stared at her.

"Oh dear," Delia exclaimed.

"How did you learn this?" Fanny asked.

"I cannot say," Georgette said. "I overheard something, by chance."

"So, these Frenchmen, the ones you just followed, they intend to pay the Englishman for this document?" Fanny asked.

Georgette nodded. "I believe it's taken them some time to gather the funds."

"And they are going to make the exchange at the ball, in the Rose Room," Fanny said.

"That is what I heard," Delia said.

"There is just one small problem," Georgette said. "It's as you said earlier today. There are balls every night."

Fanny groaned again. "And they all have Rose Rooms."

Georgette nodded.

Mr. Rupert Fellows approached. "Might I request the pleasure of a dance, Miss Markham?"

Georgette could tell that Fanny wanted to continue discussing what she and Delia had overheard. Georgette herself was still trying to understand it. But Fanny, recognizing that the gentleman who stood in front of her was a good one, smiled.

"I would like that, very much," she said.

"I promise to not step on your feet this time," he said.

Georgette could hear Fanny's gay laugh. "Oh, Mr. Fellows," she said, "Don't make promises you cannot keep."

16

$\mathcal{T}$he Duke of Eversley's head was sore. He stared at the bed curtains, which some understanding servant had been kind enough to draw. He pulled one of them aside, blinking at the light. What time was it? He sighed. He was too old to drink this much.

"You are too old to drink this much." Blanche stood by his bedside in all her ethereal beauty.

"You're back." He stared at her, drinking her in. She was dressed in a nightgown, covered with a wrapper. Her curls tumbled down her back.

She looked less clear than before. Perhaps it was the sunlight. He turned his head, trying to block out some of it.

"Not for long," she said. "I merely wished to chastise you. *Imbecile.* Why must you always be so, how do you say? Bull-headed?"

"I am not," he said. "How am I bull-headed?"

"Hah, let me count the ways." She ticked them off with

her fingers. "You refused to rest properly when you were injured."

"I did once I arrived in Vienna."

"You continue drinking and gambling all night, simply to prove a point," she said.

"I was assigned to follow Merry," he said.

"You were wallowing, *mon Chéri*. Merry must make up his own mind. You know this. Instead you left that poor lady without an escort."

"I have no doubt Miss Quinby and her cousin managed. They are both extremely resourceful young women. And I sent my regrets."

She looked at him sadly.

"You refuse to let me go," she said.

A lump rose in his throat. He squeezed his eyes.

"I cannot," he said.

"How long must I stay?" she asked sadly.

"I cannot let you go, Dear Blanche. I cannot forget."

"Letting me go does not mean forgetting me," she said. "It does not mean that you betray me, or the love we had. *Mon Chéri*, you will always love me; I know this. I was your first love, and you were mine. But it was a man ten years younger who loved me. You are different now. You will continue to change. It is not a bad thing, to find someone else to change with."

"I do not want to find someone else," he said. "I want you."

She reached out, as if to smooth away the hair from his forehead, but there were no fingers to touch his brow.

"You see? Bull-headed," she said. He closed his eyes and she was gone.

The Mad Heiress and the Duke

17

The ladies gathered in their sitting room the following afternoon. The original plan had involved a very early meeting. Unfortunately, the splendors of Vauxhall did not allow for an early return home. It had been nearly dawn by the time they returned, full of arrack punch and fireworks and music and intrigue. Comforted by the knowledge that balls never occurred before evening, the three decided that indulging in sleep would be acceptable.

Georgette suspected that Eversley would have insisted on an early meeting. He tended towards more intense behavior. His insistence on devoting himself to a life of espionage against the French after the death of his wife was a prime example.

She respected it. She understood it. How could she begrudge him this decision? He had loved Her Grace. It had been apparent in their every interaction, even for the young lady she had been. When she had seen them together, she had dreamt that she and Sebastien would one day share such a love.

That dream had well and fully died. Fortunately, Georgette reflected, she had not. She rubbed a hand on her hip, trying to ease the slight ache. While she had not danced at Vauxhall, there had been a considerable amount of activity; walking up and down the paths, watching the orchestra, sitting in a boat.

Georgette, seated at the delicate desk, set her writing materials in front of her. She dipped her pen into the ink.

"We must approach this methodically," she told the other two ladies, who were seated on one of the settees.

"Right," Fanny said. "A list of balls."

"And a list of Rose Rooms," Georgette said.

"But, how can we possibly know of everyone with a Rose Room?" Delia asked.

"We cannot," Georgette conceded. "I know of very few. But if we narrow down to the balls taking place over the next several days, we can then make inquiries as to whether or not the hosts have Rose Rooms."

"And how do you plan on making these inquiries?" Delia asked. "We cannot tell anyone what we are about."

Georgette grinned. "What do three heiresses in Town do every day?" she asked.

"Shop?" Delia suggested.

"Visit other ladies," Fanny said.

"Ride in Hyde Park," Georgette offered.

"Eat at Gunter's." This last one, Fanny delivered with a smile.

"Precisely," Georgette said. "Very well, let us begin." She motioned to a stack of invitations which she had placed on the table in front of Fanny and Delia. "If you two go through the invitations and read out the ones taking place this week, at someone's home, we can make a list."

"But how will we know that this is all the invitations?" Delia worried.

"There are benefits to being a figure of gossip," Georgette said wryly. "I do believe we managed to receive invitations to just about every social event to be held over the next week." Her lips quirked. "Many of them were delivered about a week ago."

"Shortly after Georgette's new closeness with the Duke of Eversley was discovered by the *Ton*," Fanny told Delia. "Inevitably the hostesses expressed their regret that somehow, through no fault of their own, our earlier invitation had been mislaid. If there are any events to which we have not been invited, I shall be very much surprised. But we can always make subtle and discrete inquiries when we are asking about Rose Rooms later today."

Delia looked between the two of them. "I declare," she said. "You two should consider work for the Crown."

Fanny's eyes brightened eagerly. Georgette cleared her throat. Then motioned to the two young ladies. "Well? Start reading."

"Oh, right." Fanny reached for the first in the stack. Delia followed suit.

"Marchmane ball, Thursday," Fanny read aloud. Georgette nodded and wrote it down.

"Ellicott Musicale?" Delia offered.

Georgette tapped her quill against her list. "The word

the Frenchman used. Could it have included musicale?" she asked Delia.

Delia shook her head. "No, they would have said during the musicale."

"Then let us leave that off," Georgette said. "We will only deal with the balls."

"Fletcher masquerade?" Fanny asked. She waved the invitation at Delia. "See here," she said, pointing to the additional line the lady had added. "Lady Fletcher would like to express her regret that her earlier invitation appeared to have been placed in the wrong stack, and hopes to see us there."

Georgette wrote it down. It was possible that someone would simply call that a ball, as opposed to a masquerade.

"The Prentiss ball?" Delia offered. "No, wait. It's being held in assembly rooms. So it cannot be that one."

Georgette drew a line through it. They continued through the pile of invitations until they had a list. Ten balls were being held over the course of the next week, in private residences in London.

"There," Georgette said, looking over the list. "Now we must do what we do best."

THE PARK WAS busy this afternoon. Eversley could see a number of carriages making their way around the Ring.

He'd needed the air. After a night of imbibing and gambling, he hoped that the chill of winter might help to clear his head. And indeed, he did feel better. But not entirely assuaged of guilt.

In the clear light of the following day, his note to Miss Quinby seemed somewhat lacking; to send it so late in the day. Surely, she would understand. He had important business. He was a Duke. But he might have delivered it with a touch more feeling. After all, he did not wish to sever their friendship. He did like the woman. Was that all it was, friendship?

Another gentleman came trotting up alongside him.

"Ah, Brockton," Eversley said. He nodded at the lord.

"Eversley," Brockton said. "Glad to see your head does not appear as sore as mine."

The Duke laughed. "Oh, I dare say it does. I just conceal it. It is my duty as Duke."

"And does your duty as Duke include stopping by Parliament any time soon?" Brockton asked.

He pulled up his horse. How dare Brockton question him? As a Duke, he was the one who decided when and how he devoted his time.

"It seems the right thing to do," he heard Miss Quinby say. She had said it several days ago, when he had stopped by to ask her about what she had overheard, and they had spent the afternoon talking. He had mentioned the duties he should assume, and expressed his lack of desire to attend, to dive into the politics and intrigue of Parliament.

She had looked at him seriously. "By all accounts, you appear to be a man who does the right thing," she had said. "And it seems the right thing to do."

He glowered at Brockton. "Damn it," he said. "I should

be angry with you. I am angry with you, I will have you know. Questioning me. But, consider me duly chastened." He nodded. "I will be there on the morrow."

Brockton smiled. "Very good, Your Grace," he said. "I shall not keep you any longer. I saw Miss Quinby and her cousin further along the way. No doubt I am preventing you from reaching them." He trotted away.

Miss Quinby was here? Well, that was not an especially great surprise, he had to admit. It felt as if all of Town was here, in the Park today. And Miss Quinby had an almost alarming knack for appearing wherever it was one needed her.

He nudged his horse back into a trot. He would just say hello. It would allow him to once more express his regrets over yesterday, and ensure that there were no hard feelings.

He could see the ladies, seated in their carriage. They had pulled up alongside a carriage contain Miss Prentiss and the three Smith sisters.

"Yes, we've discussed it thoroughly, and we've decided to declare it the Rose Room," Miss Markham was saying to one of the Smith sisters. "Although I suppose that isn't terribly original. Delia tells me nearly everyone has a Rose Room."

"It's true," Miss Ditherfield chimed in. "Both of my aunts have Rose Rooms."

The Smith sisters blinked. "We haven't a Rose Room," the youngest said, uncertainly.

Miss Quinby turned to Miss Prentiss. "Have you a Rose Room?" she asked the young lady.

Miss Prentiss appeared to consider. "We've a sitting

room, papered with roses?" she offered. "But no one ever uses it."

"I suppose that might do," Miss Markham said. She turned and spotted him. "Oh, Your Grace." She bowed her head. Her tone was markedly cool. "Have you a Rose Room?" she asked him.

He looked at Miss Quinby. Her cousin could not seriously be asking him about his rooms, could she?

Miss Quinby smiled. "Fanny and I are planning our redecorating. But we fear everyone else already has a Rose Room, and it simply would not do to follow in quite so many footsteps. I mean, honestly, it's as if everyone has a Rose Room. The Marchmanes, the..."

"The Marchmanes haven't got a Rose Room," one of the other Smith sisters said. "They've only a Blue Room and a Violet Room."

"Are you quite certain?" Miss Markham asked. "I truly believed they had a Rose Room."

"No," the young sister said. She appeared quite pleased to be able to impart this information. "I've been all though out their house. No Rose Room, perhaps you mistook the Violet Room."

"Perhaps," Miss Quinby said thoughtfully.

What had he stumbled into? Was this how ladies always spoke? Who could possibly care about Rose Rooms or Violet Rooms? He looked at Miss Quinby, waiting for her to smile and let him in on the joke. Instead, she had discretely pulled out a piece of paper, and appeared to be scratching out an item on a list. She looked up into his eyes, and gave a cool smile. Just like her cousin.

"You did not say," she said, "whether or not you had a Rose Room, Your Grace."

"Er, no," he said. "We've a Blue Room, which is actually decorated in a shade of rose."

Miss Quinby nodded sagely. "So often the case," she said. Then she turned back to the other ladies, who had been silently watching their exchange.

"There are so many others," she said, "are there not, Fanny? For example, what of the Fletchers?"

Miss Prentiss nodded. "Oh, that is true," she said. "They've a Rose Room, to be sure. Lady Fletcher always insists on the finest decoration."

"Too true," Miss Markham said. "She does. I have never seen the Rose Room at the Fletcher mansion, I must admit. But perhaps we shall sneak a peek of it, at their ball. Whereabouts in the mansion is it located? Somewhere I might possibly slip off to? Just for ideas, mind you..."

"Fanny!" Miss Quinby sounded outraged. But Eversley could not help noticing that, from what he could tell, she was not actually upset. She turned to the other young ladies. "Do not encourage her," she said.

"Oh no," the Smith sisters said.

"But," one of the sisters said. "If you were to, say, be on the second floor."

"Off to left," the middle sister supplied.

"Facing south," the last sister said.

"You might find it," the first sister said.

Fanny smiled at them. "Don't tell Georgette," she said in a stage whisper.

The sisters, and Miss Prentiss, all laughed.

Eversley watched as Miss Markham turned to Miss Quinby. He looked at Miss Quinby. There. She'd just winked at her cousin. She was not upset with the little chit, quite the contrary

"Well," Miss Quinby said. "We've kept you young ladies for far too long, going on about rooms. No doubt you are drowning in boredom. We will let you go. But you must come for a visit, sometime next week. And Miss Prentiss, please do tell your mother we look forward to the ball."

She turned to him. "Your Grace, it was lovely to see you."

She gave him a cool smile, and then directed the driver to carry on, leaving Eversley in the middle of Hyde Park on his horse, wondering what on earth could be so important about the color of rooms, and why he wished Miss Quinby had favored him with a better smile.

Part 4

The Rose Room Rout

18

*M*iss Georgette Quinby knew she should tell the Duke of Eversley what she and the other women discovered at Vauxhall about the spy. It was the right thing to do. It was the patriotic thing to do. She should put aside the petty hurt she had experienced when he stood her up, and she should write to him.

Georgette punched the lovely embroidered pillow sitting next to her and sniffed. She did not want to write to him.

Who did he think he was? Leaving her and Fanny without an escort, excepting Mr. Rupert Fellows, of course, who had turned out to be a lovely surprise, and one, Georgette secretly hoped would continue to woo Fanny. The man certainly had resources on a moment's notice.

Then the Duke had come riding up upon them in the park as if he had done nothing wrong, without with a so much as by-your-leave. Never mind that he was a Duke, he had no right to treat her so. She should be angry. No. She *was* angry, and hurt. Mostly, she was hurt. She punched the pillow again. She would not cry.

Georgette had thought there was something between them, at least friendship, between her and the Duke. Surely, they had friendship, but now, she didn't know what their relationship should be. She only knew what she wanted it to be....What it could not be. Had she not said she would never give her heart again after Sebastien? Had she not learned her lesson? What was she doing?

Georgette took a deep breath. She was an Englishwoman. For King and Country, she could do nothing less than her patriotic duty. There was no help for it. She had to write to the Duke. Yes. It was only duty. Then she would wash her hands of him. She would be done with him, and spying, and excitement, and the whole blasted lot. Her heart beat a quick tattoo at the thought.

If only she had not overheard the Frenchman at Vauxhall. If only Delia had not been there to translate. Then she could have happily never communicated with him again, and life would be miserable. But no matter, life could not be lived according to "if only." If it could, she would have long ago said, "if only" Sebastien had loved her; "if only" she had not fallen down the stair, and she supposed, with a sigh, Eversley would be saying "if only" too.

"If only" Blanche had not gone to France. "If only" Blanche had not been killed by the French rabble. Georgette had no right to wallow in self-pity. She was alive. She was English, and she could not let a spy have the upper hand. She would carry on. She had to get the thing done, and she would do it. She sniffled once and stood.

Georgette walked over to the delicate writing desk tucked up against the wall and searched methodically for her paper and ink. Men had studies. They had whole rooms devoted to their business. Big desks weighed down by correspondence. She had no doubt the Duke sat in an ample leather chair behind a large slab of wood whenever he had matters to attend to, where everything was in its place, but she had no such luxury.

Women had delicate writing desks with tiny drawers that didn't fit the smallest of her books or full sized pieces of parchment. It did not matter if the woman was helping to catch spies from France, if they were managing estates or funds. Business was conducted on spindly legs.

She quickly dashed out the note, keeping it deliberately vague in case it should fall into the wrong hands. Hopefully Eversley would call on her once he received it, and she could explain it all in detail.

She was almost certain that the Rose Room meeting would be at the Fletcher Masquerade. It fit the criteria: a ball and a Rose Room. The ball was in a few days, and fortunately she and Fanny had been invited, even if it was a delayed invitation only issued when they had become of interest to the *Ton*. She did not personally know the Fletchers. Fanny claimed a passing acquaintance with the younger son, but had nothing especially favorable to say about the young man. If Georgette had not been noticed by the Duke, she would not have been invited to the ball at all. Luckily...or unluckily, she was invited. She folded the note, and sealed it, well aware that correspondence between two members of the opposite sex would be cause for scandal, but she could see no help for it. England was at stake. The spy must be caught.

She called for a footman and requested the note be delivered to the Duke. His face was schooled to stillness, but she caught the censure in his eyes. No doubt the servants would gossip. Miss is passing clandestine notes to the Duke, they would say. She's gone and done it again, gone and fallen in love with a man who does not love her. She is making a fool of herself, setting her heart out on a platter for someone who will never want it. She is old enough to know better, and she was.

Well, she still had her pride. She might have fallen in love with the Duke, much to her dismay, but he did not need to know that. No one needed to know it. She would never embarrass herself again. She would tell him about the Frenchmen and the Fletcher Ball and that would be the end of it all. Georgette sucked in a sustaining breath. Perhaps they would not go to the Fletcher Ball at all. There were other outings where Fanny could see and be seen. She knew that the Duke would go to the ball to catch the spy, but there was no need for her to be seen with the Duke. She and Fanny would simply be elsewhere. She would guard her heart, even if it was a little late to be guarding.

JAMES ENTERED the Duke's study, carrying a note on a

platter. "A correspondence was just delivered, Your Grace," he said.

"Put it there," Eversley replied gesturing to the corner of the massive desk. There was little space among the Duke's papers, but James managed.

Eversley took the note absently. He was thinking about the spy.

Since determining that it was not Merry Meryton, Eversley had pulled James and Joseph off of their duties following him. He figured that if he showed himself to be at Merry's side during the afternoons and evenings, it was enough. Unfortunately, he had no idea who he should be following in Merry's stead. He stood holding the note and James waited.

He just wished Merry would stop gambling so much. The man never lost an exceptional amount; he at least seemed to be capable of reining himself in before he dug himself into a truly impossible hole. But it was all he did, every evening. Eversley looked forward to the day Mr. White called him off the case.

In the meantime, he had agreed to show his face in Parliament, and begin attending to some of his more ducal duties. He had to admit that this was not all bad. He was somewhat embarrassed that he had neglected his responsibilities for so long. Now, at long last, he could begin to rectify this.

Even if the list was recovered, he knew his days as a spy were coming to an end. It was time to become a Duke.

"From whom did it come?" he asked James, regarding the note.

"Miss Quinby, I believe," James said.

"I see," he said, "Thank you, James."

The servant recognized the dismissal and left the Duke alone. Had James expected the Duke to pen a reply?

He stared at the note. Miss Quinby. His heart leapt at hearing she had sent him a note. She had acted so coolly to him in the park, and he had been taken aback by how much that had bothered him. But now she was sending him notes? It was quite improper. What was she on about?

He knew he should not have abandoned her without an escort at the last minute. It was unacceptably rude. But surely now she understood that, despite their moment of closeness, there could be nothing between him. Sending him a note, however, reeked of desperation.

He stared at it, and placed it back on the silver salver James had left behind.

Best to just ignore it. Save her dignity. Nothing could come of their acquaintance.

19

*F*anny was in Georgette's room, fairly bouncing on her bed in excitement. "Wake up, Georgette. Wake up. Today is the day!"

Georgette slowly blinked awake and groaned. "Fanny, I see no reason why you need wake me at this hour. The ball is not until this evening. Let me sleep."

"I can't," Fanny said. "I am simply aquiver with excitement."

Georgette rolled over to stare at her young cousin. "Why can you not be aquiver without my company? I will join you later, after another hour or so of sleep."

Fanny walked over and tugged the bedclothes down. "We've much to do," she said. "We've outfits to plan, and strategy to discuss."

"We have already planned out ball gowns," Georgette said. "And we've discussed so much strategy, I have even started dreaming of it."

Georgette closed her eyes again. "Besides," she said, "it is a relatively simple plan."

And it was. The ladies had decided that Georgette would hide in the study. Fanny would hide outside of it, while Delia would keep an eye out for anything amiss at the ball. There had been some disagreement about the roles; Delia and Fanny felt they should be doing something more, but Georgette prevailed. She didn't want the younger girls involved with anything that might cause scandal. Her reputation was already in tatters. Hers did not matter so much.

"I still wish I was hiding with you," Fanny said.

"I told you, we need you to be stationed outside, to provide a distraction or sound the alarm if need be," Georgette said.

Fanny let out a huff. "Any word from Eversley?" she asked.

Georgette shook her head. She had lowered herself even further yesterday, by stopping to call at his residence, and asked to wait in the drawing room while the butler inquired.

The residence had been just as Georgette remembered. Decorated exquisitely and tastefully, it was an ode to Her Grace. The Duchess had been known for her remarkable ability to decorate, Georgette remembered.

Many of the *Ton* decorated in the latest style. Each Season was an excuse for new drapery, new wall paper, new upholstery. Greek and Roman motifs, gilded furniture, china figurines.

Georgette had long stopped paying attention to the

latest trends. When she was sixteen and in love, she had decorated many a room in her head. The room where she and Sebastien would eat their supper, the room where she would do her sewing, the room where she would play her music and Sebastien would sit, entranced. Then Sebastien had run away with the Duke's sister, and decorating imaginary rooms lost its appeal. Why spend time decorating a room when Sebastien would never sit in it?

Then, as the years passed, she had stopped bothering with trends altogether, simply because she did not see the point. If she was to be a spinster, she wanted to exist for the rest of her life in spaces she enjoyed. She did not care about fashion. She cared about comfort. When she agreed to join Fanny in Town, she had left all the decorating decisions to her cousin, who was decidedly *a la mode*.

The Duke's residence was not fashionable. Even Georgette could recognize that it was ten years out of date. But it remained comfortable and pleasant, filled with enjoyable and beautiful things. Just like Blanche.

For a moment, as she had stood in the Duke's drawing room yesterday, she had fancied she could see Her Grace. She was standing by the mantle, smiling at Georgette, a mischievous look in her eyes. What would she say to her, if she were there? *Your husband still mourns you. He will never love another. And yet, I think I may be falling in love with him. I'm so sorry, Your Grace. I did not plan it.*

And what would Her Grace say back? The Blanche she had known, so briefly, all those years ago; what would she have said? Georgette liked to think that perhaps Her

Grace would smile and tell her that it was a good thing, that he needed someone to love, and be loved by, that people could not be forever trapped by the tragedies of long ago.

She looked back over at the mantel piece. The vision of the lady was gone. A throat cleared and Georgette looked up from her wool gathering.

"I beg your pardon, Miss Quinby." The butler gave a short bow. "His Grace is unfortunately not at home."

Georgette was stunned. She stared at the butler for a full minute before she gathered her wits.

Georgette lay back in bed, thinking of the hot blush of embarrassment she had felt, the sympathetic smile of the butler.

His Grace had been home, but ignored her. What did he think she was there for? To throw herself at him, like some sort of harlot? The fact that he thought so angered her.

Very well, she had thought, as she swept from his drawing room. Let him treat her so callously. She did not need him to save her country. She did not need him to care for her. She could do it on her own.

Georgette looked at Fanny, who was still in her bedroom, looking like a sad-eyed hound, eager for the hunt to begin.

"Oh bother," Georgette said. "I suppose I won't be getting any more sleep. You may as well ring for some chocolate."

Fanny bounced on the bed again and hugged her cousin.

Rokesby, the Duke's butler, stood in doorway. "Merry Meryton is waiting downstairs, Your Grace." He said smoothly.

Eversley looked up. Rokesby had been giving him mildly reproving looks for the last day, ever since Miss Quinby had come for a visit and he had refused her.

"Do you wish me to tell him you are not at home?" Rokesby asked, stiffly. The note of censure was unmistakable. Eversley ignored it.

Eversley sighed and pushed back from his desk. "No," he said. "No, I will go see what Merry wants."

Merry was standing in the entryway, slapping his hat against his leg.

"Ah, Eversley," he said, as the Duke descended. "Get your hat and coat."

Eversley blinked. "Am I going somewhere?" he asked.

Merry nodded and shrugged. "Seeing as no matter where I go, you are bound to show up; I decided to call upon you before heading to the club. Saves you the effort of tracking me down, old boy."

"Was I so very obvious?" Eversley asked.

Merry snorted. "I don't particularly care for your meddling," he said, "although I appreciate that it comes from good intentions."

Eversley forbore stating that it had actually not stemmed from good intentions at all. He had originally believed Merry to be a traitor to the Crown. He motioned with his head to Joseph, who ran lightly up the stairs to retrieve his things.

"You could save me the effort altogether," he said to Merry, "and stop gambling."

Merry snorted. "Coming from the man who could do whatever he wished."

Eversley bristled. "I cannot do everything I might wish," he said.

"I beg your pardon," Merry said, and he sounded genuinely sorry. "I did not mean to suggest that you have not experienced loss. I simply meant to point out that should you ever decide to do anything; woo another woman, travel the world, build a bloody castle, you could do it. You have the means and the ability."

"Merry, I am fortunate, I know this. If all you needed was funds, I would gladly give you the money..."

"I am not a charity case." Merry's voice was suddenly low and dangerous.

"I never said you were."

For a long moment, Merry stared at him. "I'm going to the club," he said. "And I will gamble until I win, or until my funds are entirely depleted. And you shall not stop me, Eversley. I will accept the companionship, but I will not accept anything else. If you wish to offer something more, you can go find Miss Quinby. Rumor is she's desperate for you."

"Careful, Merry, or I should call you out," Eversley said.

A smile crossed Merry's lips. "Good," he said.

Joseph returned with Eversley's coat and hat and sword cane, which he had taken to carrying years ago when he first began his work in France. Eversley accepted them silently, still seething over Merry's words regarding Miss Quinby.

Yes, she was desperate for him. He knew this. Two notes and a visit? Lud, the woman should have some dignity. He'd just paid her a modicum of attention. He'd visited a couple of times, and sent her some music. That was all. He should not have sent the music.

Yes, he had found himself frequently thinking how nice it would be to tell Miss Quinby about the events of his life, about his visits to Parliament and about Merry and about the little moments of his day which brought him joy and sadness. But that did not mean anything. It had simply been nice, that was all. It was nice to have a friend.

And yes, once or twice he had allowed himself to envision her as more, to consider how it might feel to be able to reach out and touch her cheek, to allow his hand to settle possessively on the small of her back, to be with her as a man. But that was simply loneliness. That was simply being in this house, alone.

Without Blanche.

$\mathcal{T}$he Fletcher Masquerade was one of the Great Events of the Season, according to Fanny, who had it on good authority from the Smith sisters. Mrs. Fletcher had hosted the ball for the past five years, and every year it became more and more extravagant. Ladies and gentlemen of the *Ton* were known to spend months planning their costumes. The sheer amount of feathers and jewels and satin and velvet that went to one single night was astonishing.

Georgette had elected to wear a simple domino, much to Fanny's dismay. She had only been allowed her "incredibly boring and dismal" costume after she had pointed out to Fanny that one could not easily hide in cupboards in Rose Rooms if one was dressed as a swan. Fanny, on the other hand, was dressed as a magnificent peacock, with a beaded skirt and an astonishment of feathers.

"I know, I know," she said. "I'm dressed as a male

peacock. But I wasn't about to go as a female, although no doubt wearing a large brown sack would be slightly more comfortable. Who knew beading was so heavy?" She shifted her shoulder and grimaced.

"You look wonderful," Georgette said.

Mr. Rupert Fellows promptly arrived to escort them. He too had gone for the simple domino.

"I once attempted to dress as a knight of the realm," he explained to the ladies as he handed them up into the carriage. "But my breastplate fell off during the jig and injured my companion."

Fanny patted his arm. "Best to leave the extravagant costumes to others," she said soothingly.

He nodded. "I should probably keep a wide berth of your costume." He shuddered. "All that beading."

Fanny nodded, but did not look overly thrilled by the idea of Mr. Fellows not being nearby.

"Perhaps best if I skirt you entirely."

"Why, Mr. Fellows, your wordplay astonishes me," Fanny said.

Mr. Fellows grinned. Georgette glanced over to Fanny, who was trying to hide her smile.

The ride to the ball took no time at all. The Fletcher mansion was only two squares over. They also managed to avoid the normally excruciating wait to disembark, as they had arrived very early. A fact Mr. Fellows remarked upon.

"Deuced early," he said.

"I like to arrive promptly," Fanny said. "To spend as much time as possible."

Mr. Fellows nodded, as if this was an entirely

reasonable statement. Georgette sent up a silent thanks that Mr. Fellows appeared to be willing to serve Fanny's every whim.

The three of them entered the ballroom, Georgette and Fanny on Mr. Fellow's arms. Georgette scanned those assembled. Very few guests were at the ball. They milled about in small groups, sipping on punch, eyeing each other's costumes and comparing extravagance.

Mr. Fellows murmured about finding the ladies refreshments, and left them near one of the mantels, by a fire. The room was not yet filled with people, and so that warmth of the fire was appreciated. An orchestra was stationed at the other end of the room, but they were not yet playing dances.

"Any sign of the Frenchman?" Fanny asked.

Georgette skimmed once more over the ball guests and shook her head. "No," she said. "I believe I should make my excuses and go to the retiring room. It would not do to have the Frenchman arrive before I am in place."

Fanny nodded. They had discussed this before the ball. Georgette would retire to mend a hem, and then hide herself in the Rose Room. Fanny would distract Mr. Fellows. Hopefully Delia would soon arrive, and she could also scan the ball guests.

"Go," Fanny said. "Before he returns with our drinks."

Georgette squeezed her cousin's hand and made her way out of the ballroom.

What had the Smith sisters said?

"If you were to, say, be on the second floor."

"Off to left."

173

"Facing South."

"You might find it."

She trod silently down the carpeted hallways, her slippers making barely a sound. Past sitting rooms and blue rooms and gold rooms.

There. The Rose Room.

It was dark, just one lamp was lit. No one appeared to be in the room. She made her way around, poking her head under tables and into cabinets, ensuring no one was there. It was deserted.

Where could she hide? It had to be somewhere comfortable. Who knew how long she would be there. There was the side table over on the right side, the long lace covering would likely keep her from view. There was the lacquered Chinese trunk in the middle of the room. She raised the lid. It was mercifully empty, but also very dirty. And both of these were bound to be cramped, and make any sudden escapes or movements impossible.

She looked about in frustration. There had to be somewhere.

Hmmmm. She peered at the long heavy drapes that flanked the windows. She could hide behind those, but no doubt they would notice her bulk. But if she drew a chair in front, it might seem less noticeable.

Well, she supposed that was the only option. She may as well give it a try.

She untied one of the drapes, and then dragged over one of the lighter, balloon-backed chairs in front of it. Carefully, trying not to disturb the chair, she slid behind the curtains. She hoped her slippers were not visible. Hopefully, the lights would remain relatively unlit.

Time to wait.

THE CLUB WAS NOT OVERCROWDED this evening, as Eversley and Merry made their way in. Why was he here? Why did he follow Merry? The man had insulted him, his honor, and Miss Quinby. He should let Merry ruin himself.

Merry aimed for one of the higher stakes tables. Normally, he confined himself to the lower stakes, never trusting himself with too much money; never having enough to lose. Tonight, however, he was even more reckless.

He stared aggressively back at Eversley, daring the Duke to tell him not to play. But Eversley remained silent. Instead he wandered over to the window, staring out the wavy glass onto the rainy street below, at the horses standing in the mud. From this vantage point, he could see the pedestrians and carriages that turned into the street, rounding a corner not too far away.

Merry continued to play. Most of the gentlemen at the club tonight were ones Eversley did not know. He supposed there must be some important social event that kept away the others. No doubt he had received an invitation to it. He wondered if he had accepted.

"A hundred pounds." It was Lord Bramblehurst. He and Mr. Turner had entered the room.

Mr. Turner chuckled. "I heard you the first time, Bramblehurst, and it's a fool's bet, I tell you. I only make bets with the chance I can win."

Lord Bramblehurst grunted. "Thirteen," he said.

Mr. Turner waved him off. "Pick a different bet," he said.

Lord Bramblehurst turned to the Duke. "What say you?" he asked, his jowls waggling like a bulldog's. "Interested in the bet?"

"What are you betting?" Eversley asked.

"A thousand to guess what the next person who comes around that corner looks like," Bramblehurst said.

Eversley laughed and shook his head.

"Five," Bramblehurst said, as if increasing the amount would increase the temptation. " Five thousand pounds. If you get the sex and color of dress correct. That's not so hard is it?"

Eversley smiled. "You must forgive me, Bramblehurst," he said, "but that's not a bet for me."

The lord raised his voice. "Is there no one in this bloody club interested in my bet?"

"I'll take it."

Heads turned. It was Merry. He was staring at Lord Bramblehurst. Then his gaze slid to the Duke, again daring him to stop him.

Eversley started. What was Merry doing? Then he stopped himself. Let him lose, he thought. Let him destroy it all. At least it would mercifully be over.

He stared back at Merry and shrugged.

Bramblehurst grinned and rubbed his hands together. "Capital," he said. "Five?"

Merry nodded.

"And what do you think the person shall be?" he asked.

Merry thought for a moment. "A lady," he said. "Green coat over a plum dress. And your wager?"

"Gentleman," Bramblehurst said. "Navy coat, top hat."

He held out his hand. Merry shook it. They walked to the window and peered out.

"Any moment," Bramblehurst said. "Someone will turn the corner at any...ah."

The room was hushed, as the other occupants waited to hear what they saw.

"It's a woman," Merry said.

Lord Bramblehurst blinked. "With a green coat," he said.

Silence. Eversley could hear rain against the window.

"Over a plum dress," Merry said, the astonishment in his voice evident.

"What?" One of the other gentlemen finally spoke. "I say, Merry, does this mean you've won?"

Merry blinked. "I..." he said. "Yes." He gave a little laugh. "I suppose I have."

The room erupted with laughter. Merry Meryton, winning the gamble!

Lord Bramblehurst was looking decidedly uneasy. Eversley imagined that he never actually had to pay up on his bets. However, Merry would no doubt be requesting immediate payment. Five thousand pounds would solve a multitude of Merry's problems.

After the noise had died down somewhat, and several gentlemen had stopped by to slap Merry on the back, Merry turned to Lord Bramblehurst.

"I believe you owe me," he said, holding out his hand. "Five pounds."

Eversley wanted to laugh. Five? Merry had clearly misspoken.

"Ah," Lord Bramblehurst fingered his cravat. "Might take me some time," he said.

"Oh, never matter," Merry said. "You've got credit here, have you not? Simply tell them to give me five pounds of it."

A second time, he'd left off the thousand. Eversley looked at Merry, questioningly. What was the man doing?

Lord Bramblehurst looked equally confused. "Young man," he said. "It takes time to transfer those funds. I must see my solicitor, and my banker." Sweat began to trickle down his temple.

Merry set a hand on his shoulder. "No," he said. "We wagered five pounds. You asked five, and we shook on it. That's all you owe me."

Lord Bramblehurst's mouth silently formed the word: Five. Five pounds. Not five thousand.

Merry smiled. "You can pay me the next time we see one another," he said. "In the meantime, I've a ball to attend."

Eversley was hot on his heels as he strode out of the club. "What in the blazes are you doing, man?" he demanded.

Merry shrugged. "Delia told me she would be at the Fletcher Masquerade."

"Delia," Eversley said. "Delia Ditherfield? The reason you've been throwing your money away in gambling halls? That Delia?"

Merry nodded.

"The Delia you could be proposing to with five

thousand pounds in your pocket right now? That Delia?" Eversley could hear his own voice rising. "Did you not realize you won five thousand pounds, not five, Merry?"

Merry stopped to look in either direction, to avoid the horses; then led them across the street.

"I realized. I also realized I could not go to her like that," he said. "That if I came to her with five thousand pounds from a fool's bet, I'd be no better than a fool. I would always be thinking that I could solve the problem, with just a bit more money, a bit more luck."

"Bramblehurst is good for it," Eversley said. "He just needed to get to his solicitor. He did make the bet."

"I know, but that isn't the point is it?" He turned the corner and they made their way through the London streets, toward the Fletcher residence.

"What is the point then?" Eversley asked.

"Love," Merry said. "Love, old boy. But you knew that all along didn't you?" He slapped Eversley on the back.

The residence was illuminated by thousands of candles, beaming out into the darkness. Carriages lined the streets, slowly moving forward to empty their occupants. Eversley could hear the strains of the music playing within, the laughter.

"She's worth more than that," Merry said. "Delia is worth more than a bit of luck."

He moved forward, pushing through the carriages and up the stairs. The two men were evidently undressed for a masquerade ball, but one mention of the Duke's name gave them access.

Delia Ditherfield was standing in the corner. She appeared to be intently scanning the crowd through her mask. When her eyes fell on Merry, she stilled. He walked forward and took her hand and bowed over it.

"Miss Ditherfield," he said. "I've been an ass."

She looked down upon his head. "Yes," she said. "Yes, you have been."

He looked up. "Will you do me the honor of becoming my wife?" he asked.

Miss Ditherfield smiled. "I will," she said. "I love you dearly. But right now, I'm afraid I'm slightly distracted."

Merry straightened. Eversley could tell he was slightly astonished that Miss Ditherfield had not leapt into his arms, sobbing.

"Er," Merry said. "What seems to be amiss?"

"I'm assisting Miss Markham and Miss Quinby," Miss Ditherfield said.

Eversley, who had begun to turn away, he was not especially concerned with Merry's betrothed's distractions, stopped. He turned back at the mention of Miss Quinby.

"Miss Markham and Miss Quinby?" he asked, trying to sound nonchalant.

Miss Ditherfield nodded. "We overheard something the other day, at Vauxhall. Well, Miss Quinby recognized the voice, but could not understand. Fortunately I speak French." She pursed her lips. "So I translated. But I should not say more," she said.

"French?" Eversley asked. "You overheard French?"

Miss Ditherfield nodded.

"Where is Miss Quinby now?" Eversley asked tightly.

Miss Ditherfield lifted her chin and looked down her nose at him.

"I believe she wrote to you," she said. "And visited. And yet, you ignored her. Why should I tell you? Do you now suddenly care for her?"

Eversley ran a hand through his hair. "I deserve it, I know," he said. "But please, tell me. Where is she now?"

"The Frenchmen were going to meet someone," Miss Ditherfield said. "Here. At the ball."

At the ball. At the Fletcher mansion? Where?

Then he remembered: the ladies in Hyde Park, asking all sorts of questions about decoration.

"The Rose Room?" he asked.

Miss Ditherfield nodded.

"Where is she?" he demanded fearfully. "Where is Miss Quinby?"

"She's hiding," Miss Ditherfield said. "Waiting to catch them out."

"The bloody fool," Eversley said, and then dashed from the room.

21

*H*er feet were numb. Georgette carefully shifted and tried to rub the top of one of her feet with the other. She felt as if she'd been waiting for forever. Perhaps the masquerade had ended, and it was dawn, and all the guests had departed, and she was still waiting like a fool behind a curtain.

No. Fanny and Delia would have come and found her.

Wait? What was that?

It was the creak of a door. Then there was the sound of boots on the floor. The individual made their way to the fire. Soon enough, the room was much brighter; Georgette could tell by the greater glow at the base of the curtains. She held as still as possible, breathing softly and gulping in her nervousness.

There were several minutes of silence then the sound of another party entering.

"Here we are," a voice said. It was the Frenchman. Georgette could recognize the lilt of his accent.

"Let's make it quick," the Englishman said. "I need to return to the ball. I will be missed."

"But of course, *Monsieur*," the Frenchman said. "Very well, may I see the list?"

There was the sound of rustling and then a pause. "You won't have this in your hands until I see my money," the Englishman said.

"*Oui,* very well." There was the sound of something being dragged on the floor, and what she believed was a lid opening. "Like a pirate, no?" the Frenchman said. "You may count it if you like, although I must warn you, counting that much coin may take you considerable time. We will be here all night."

The other gentleman grunted.

"And so you must trust me," the Frenchman said

"I suppose that is my only choice," the Englishman said. "Very well, here is the list."

There was the sound of someone stepping forward.

"*Merci,*" the Frenchman said. Then he coughed, a strange wet sound.

What should she do? She could not let the Frenchman take it. Why had she thought she could hide in the Rose Room? What had she thought to do? In her mind it had been simple: she would suddenly leap forward and put a stop to it all. Now was her chance. She must do it. Why had she not brought a pistol or at least something with which to threaten them? She was a lone woman and she had no way to stop this, and yet, she had to.

Georgette pushed the chair forward and stepped out from behind the curtain.

"Stop..." she cried. And then the words died on her lips.

Lord Fletcher was standing in the middle of the room, holding a dagger, which he had just thrust into the Frenchman. He pulled the dagger out. The Frenchman gave one final wheezing sound and then slumped heavily to the floor, his eyes glazing.

"Well, well, well," Lord Fletcher said. "What have we here?"

It was odd, Georgette thought, how she had never actually heard Lord Fletcher speak before now. Up until this point, she had only ever seen him from afar. Although, she supposed she had heard him before. She just hadn't known it was him at the British Museum.

And now he was advancing upon her with a bloody knife.

Dozens of thoughts flashed through Georgette's mind at that moment. She wished she had brought something to defend herself with. She wished she had arranged for better back up than Fanny in her peacock outfit. She wished she had been more demanding with Eversley, that he listen to her.

She wished she had never insisted she and Delia follow and eavesdrop on the Frenchman. She wished she had never gone to the British Museum, that she had never picked up the note in the potted plant. She wished she had never fallen in love with Sebastien. She wished she had never run up those stairs, that she had never thought to die. She didn't want to die.

Not true. You don't regret any of it; except maybe death at Lord Fletcher's hands.

"Don't you dare," she said to Lord Fletcher.

He stopped for a second, likely taken aback by the audacity of an unprotected woman, telling him not to stab her. She figured it was worth trying.

"I will scream terribly loudly," she said. "You have no idea."

"No one will notice a scream," he laughed. "The din from the ballroom will drown it out."

She moved, putting the chair in between them.

"Go on," he said. "Scream." He waved the knife at her.

Good God, he was truly demented. And not afraid to murder, if the Frenchman's demise was any indication.

Then he screamed. It occurred so suddenly, Georgette barely knew what had occurred. One moment, he had been stepping towards her, knife in hand. Then there was a thin sword, slicing through the air, onto his arm. The knife he had held, clattered to the floor, and Lord Fletcher let out a terrifying, high-pitched squeal.

Georgette blinked at the knife, and at the man who was clutching his arm. She followed the tip of the sword back to the man holding it.

"Hello, Eversley," she said. She attempted to sound calm, but feared the tremble in her voice betrayed her.

His eyes were aflame. He was breathing heavily, staring at Fletcher. He pointed the sword, which he had unsheathed from his walking stick, towards the man's heart.

"Traitor," he said. His voice was low. The tip of the sword nudged up against Fletcher's heart.

"Eversley," Georgette said. "Please don't."

"Oh, I won't," he said. "As long as he keeps very

very still."

Georgette stepped forward, towards the Frenchman.

"What are you doing?" Eversley asked. "Get away from him." But he did not move, he kept his sword trained on Fletcher.

She leaned down and began rifling through the Frenchman's coat pockets, trying to ignore the fact that she was doing this to a dead man. She was carefully trying to avoid the blood. There was quite a lot of it.

"He gave it to him," she said to Eversley. "He gave him the list."

"It was likely a fake," Eversley said. "I imagine he planned to kill the man as soon as he had his money."

Ah. She found it. Carefully, she pulled it from the Frenchman's waistcoat. She unfolded it, skimming the list of names. There was Eversley. She looked up. Eversley was on the list. A list of spies. How long had the Duke been a spy for England? In France? She wondered. Was this his penance after Blanche's death? Was that why he stayed away so long?

"Well?" he said. "Can you deduce what it is?"

"What type of fool would write them all down?" she whispered horrified at the thought of what could have happened if this list fell into the wrong hands, as it very nearly did.

Eversley gave out a short laugh. "We do not question His Highness."

Fletcher moved, and then stopped.

"Don't test me, Fletcher," Eversley said. "Do. Not. Test. Me."

"Do you need it?" Georgette asked.

"Need what?" Eversley asked.

"The list," she said. What did he think she was asking about? "Do you need it?"

THE LIST? He furrowed his brow. When she had asked if he needed it, he was not entirely certain what he thought she meant. Her? Was she asking if he needed her? He did. He needed her. He had not realized just how much until he had burst in on Fletcher about to run her through with a dagger.

Was she asking if he needed Blanche? He needed Blanche, he did. She was his wife. She was his wife and he had loved her and lost her and the pain had been unbearable. He could not do that again. He could not lose another love. He could not bear it.

No, she was asking about the list. All of the spies for The Crown, gathered together into one place. A single tiny piece of paper, worthless on its face, and yet so terrifying powerful. Anyone with those names...oh, the things they could do, the lives they could destroy.

"Burn it," he said.

"Very well," she said.

He could hear the soft tread of her slippers, and then she came into view, moving towards the fire. She leaned down and tossed it in. He could see it catch fire and burst into flame.

Miss Quinby straightened. The fire illuminated her, and for a moment she looked like a vengeful angel, so different from Blanche, and yet so beautiful.

"He killed him," she said gesturing back toward the man on the floor. "Fletcher killed him."

"He was a spy for the French," Eversley said. "It was not an entire loss."

"He was a man," she said. "Fighting for his own country. And Fletcher killed him. After he had betrayed his own."

She walked over to stare down at Mr. Fletcher. "What kind of man are you?" she asked.

Fletcher stared back at her disdainfully. "So easy for you," he said. "The Mad Heiress." He laughed. "Never wanted for anything."

She looked up at Eversley. "That's not true," she said. "I've wanted." Then she looked back down at Fletcher. "What a horrible man you are, my Lord."

Fletcher snarled.

"Get up," Eversley said to the man.

Fletcher slowly raised himself up, while Eversley kept his sword trained upon him.

"There," Eversley said. "That wasn't so bad, was it?"

And then, with practiced motion, he clocked Lord Fletcher with a stiff upper cut. The man's eyes rolled back and he fell to the floor.

"Heavens!" Miss Quinby said. "Was that absolutely necessary?"

"It was if I wanted to easily tie him up," he said to her. "Can you reach for the rope holding the drapery?"

22

$\mathcal{M}$iss Quinby went to the windows and pulled the rope down. She didn't have vapors, in fact, she was remarkably cool through the whole ordeal he thought with pride. She handed the tie over to him. He carefully knotted Fletcher's hands behind him. Then he pulled off the man's cravat and used it to gag him. He drew back and stared at the two men now resting on the floor, one dead, one bound.

What was he to do with them? How was he to successfully remove them from this room without drawing suspicion? Anyone could walk in the door at any moment.

He would have to send Georgette to find Mr. Murphy. In the meantime, there was a small closet off to the side. He could remove the men there.

He turned to speak to Georgette. He could look at her, now that Fletcher was handily tied up.

"I need to send word for assistance, but am loathe to

leave Fletcher unattended, even bound," he said. "First, I need to move the men into the small closet next door. Then, if you could be so kind, as to go to my residence, which is not far and locate either Mr. Murphy, or my footmen, Joseph or James. Tell them to send word to White and then come here. That would be much appreciated."

"Send word to White?" Miss Quinby asked.

"They will understand what it means," he said to her. "But first, might you assist me with Fletcher's feet?"

The man was still out and unresponsive, but was likely to awaken at any moment. He lifted his torso and motioned to Miss Quinby, who grabbed the gentleman's feet. Carefully, they shuffled to the door. Miss Quinby set his feet down, slowly opened the door, and then peered out.

"The coast is clear," she said. "Let me open the closet first. Would be a dreadful shock if we were to open it and discover two servants, enjoying some time together."

He snorted. Leave it to Miss Quinby to be practical at a moment like this.

She ran forward and opened the closet door. The small space was blessedly empty. Together, they carried Fletcher in and closed it.

The Frenchman was more difficult. Miss Quinby covered the stain on the carpet by moving one of the decorative tables, and they were careful to keep the rest of the mess away from their clothes, but not entirely successful. Slowly, they raised the body up and began moving to the door.

Then he stopped. The noise outside the door had changed.

"Miss Quinby," he said, "I believe we might have a slight difficulty."

SLIGHT DIFFICULTY? Was the man serious? He was holding a dead body; a dead French spy, no less, after knocking out the traitor, and he was speaking of slight difficulties? She had blood on her dress, she'd almost been stabbed, and he was speaking of slight difficulties?

Then she heard it. There was a din just outside the door.

"Oh," she said. "Oh no."

Later, when asked by Fanny what prompted her to do it, Georgette would say she was not entirely certain. But the thought that had swept through her mind was that the Duke could not be seen doing this, that someone had to stop them.

She dropped the Frenchman's feet and ran.

Lady Fletcher was known for her sumptuous supper spreads, and reveled in their dramatic display. The supper hall, therefore, was closed to ballroom guests until supper was announced. The guests would then file into the hallway and up the stairs and await the dramatic opening of the doors for entry. This was what was occurring now. The guests were beginning to ascend the stairs. From the bottom of the stairs, they could see neither the Rose Room, nor the supply closet. Once at the top, at the point where they would enter the supper hall, however, the view was clear.

They would see everything.

No, Georgette thought. No.

She rushed forward to the top of the stairs, her arms outstretched, gesturing at the ball guests all to stay back.

"If you all could please stay back," she called out. "For just a few moments." She craned her head back to look at the Rose Room. She could see Eversley slowly dragging the Frenchman to the closet.

She turned back to the crowd. The mass of ball guests had frozen in shock. They stared up at her, several mouths hung open, jaws slack. It was a sea of dominoes and masks.

She still had her mask on, she thought. Perhaps they would not realize who it was.

"It's Miss Quinby!" someone said.

No such luck. She groaned.

"The Mad Heiress!" someone else called out.

"Oh God, she's going to jump!" A young girl pointed a shaking finger at Georgette.

A lady fainted.

A gentleman made to dash up the stairs towards her.

"No!" Georgette held out her hands and he paused. "No, no. Do not trouble yourself. I am not going to do any such thing."

She heard a loud thump come from the closet.

"It's the Duke!" Another voice called out from the crowd. "She's heartbroken to learn she cannot have him."

What? Was it really such public knowledge?

"I am not!" Georgette tried to locate the voice in the

crowd. "This is nothing to do with that. Please. You've all got quite the wrong idea." Not that she could tell them what was actually occurring. Then they really would think she was mad.

Dash it. What could she say to them? How could she keep them from coming up the stairs, and still maintain her dignity? It was impossible. Her dignity was gone.

"Georgette!" It was Fanny, rushing through the crowd.

"Don't let her jump!" one of the gentlemen at the foot of the stairs yelled.

"I'm not going to jump!" Georgette yelled back. "I just need you all to wait, just one moment. Supper is not quite ready."

"Supper most certainly is ready." It was Lady Fletcher. "How dare you say otherwise?"

She was standing at the foot of the stairs, escorted by the Duke of Horland. Georgette blinked down at her. She wondered if Lady Fletcher was aware her husband was a traitor, if she knew he'd taken a list of spies from the King and tried to sell it to the French for money, if she knew he was a murderer.

"Georgette." Fanny reached her side. She looked terribly concerned.

"I'm not going to jump," Georgette said. "I simply need the crowd to stop for a moment. So they would not see what happened."

Fanny nodded. "I am so sorry I could not get to you sooner," she said. "I tried to escape the ballroom, so that I might come up here, but it was nearly impossible. Delia had the same trouble. Merry wouldn't let her out of his sights and..." She trailed off as she glanced back down at the crowd, which was still staring at them, waiting for Georgette to scream and kill herself, no doubt.

Georgette looked back. The door to the closet was closed, and the Rose Room appeared deserted. Then the Duke came into view.

"Go," he mouthed. "Go. Tell my driver to find White."

"Let us go," Georgette said. "I am tired, Fanny, all of a sudden."

Fanny, who was still staring down into the crowd below, and had not noticed the Duke, nodded.

Together they slowly descended. Georgette stopped in front of Lady Fletcher.

"It was a lovely masquerade," she said. She curtseyed deeply.

The Lady glowered at her, no doubt irate that Georgette had ruined the dramatic entrance into the supper hall which she had planned.

"I certainly hope we managed to provide you with a scene," Fanny said. "Your ball will be the talk for years to come."

Lady Fletcher did appear to brighten somewhat at that thought. "There is that," she said.

The crowd parted for them, as they made their way. It was oddly silent, Georgette thought. It sounded as if she had just been tossed into a lake. She could not seem to make out any voices. She felt she was in a dream or underwater.

They exited the residence and Mr. Fellows went to inquire about their carriage.

"Why could we not have supper?" Fanny questioned. "I'm quite starved."

"We need to go to the Duke's residence first," Georgette said. "To deliver a message."

IT WAS DAWN before the Duke returned home. His footmen, James and Joseph, had arrived not long after Miss Quinby departed. Together, the three of them managed to remove the two men into a carriage. Amazingly, they avoided detection. The ball guests were still so thrilled by Miss Quinby's near suicide attempt they could speak of nothing else.

Mr. White appeared not long after. He nodded, as Eversley explained the events of the evening.

"You burned the list?" he asked. Eversley was not certain whether White was pleased or displeased about this development, but he did not particularly care.

"I did," he said. "Tell me White, how did you miss Fletcher?"

White shrugged. "Sometimes we fail," he said.

"Mmmm," Eversley said. "Sometimes we do, indeed."

It went unspoken, Eversley's resignation, but it was there all the same. He was done with espionage, with clandestine affairs. He had other responsibilities and wishes. Mr. White did not say anything, but he knew the man knew.

Miss Quinby had almost died. She had almost been killed, and it would have been his fault. His failure. He could not bear it. When he closed his eyes to sleep, all he could see was the bloody knife and her wide eyes.

He should visit her. He should stop by her residence tomorrow, and inquire as to her condition.

The guests had thought she wanted to jump. They had thought she wanted to kill herself, over him. Over a Duke she barely knew, he thought. Surely she did not love him.

He knew his feelings were stronger than he liked to admit, but surely hers were not. She was an eminently practical woman. Not like Blanche at all. He had already learned that her actions, which he had believed to be motivated by desire for him, had been in response to overhearing the Frenchman.

What were the odds? They were astonishing, he thought. Almost as astonishing as Merry naming a green coat and a plum dress.

It had to be Fate. If Miss Quinby had not been in the garden that day, he would not have remembered her. If she had not found that note, she would not have been at the British Museum. Likewise, he would not have been there if he had not been assigned to Merry as a decoy. It was Fate that led her, and apparently Delia Ditherfield, to Vauxhall and to the spies. He could not believe she had overheard another conversation.

It was Fate that had led Merry to make that bet, to realize that though he had won, he still did not have the thing which was most important to him. It was Fate which had brought Eversley along to the ball, Fate which had made Delia Ditherfield tell him Miss Quinby was hiding in the Rose Room. Fate which had brought him there, just in time, to save her before she died.

She had almost died.

He could not bear it.

He poured himself a drink and paced his bedroom.

"Blanche," he said aloud. "Where are you? I need you."

Blanche appeared as she always did and looked at him sadly. *"Pas mon idiot,"* she said.

"No?"

"Pas mon idiot que vous ne le faites pas," she repeated and disappeared again.

"I am not an idiot," he said to the empty air. He downed the drink and poured another. He scowled at the place where she had been. Whatever could Blanche have meant?

23

SIX MONTHS LATER

eorgette lay back and stared up at the leaves. It was summer, and she was in one of her favorite fields. Butterflies flew lazily about, birds sang. She could hear the rush of a small stream nearby.

She had retreated home, after that disastrous time in London, to lick her wounds. Not only had she been in a mild state of shock, after seeing a man killed, she had been hurt and embarrassed. The *Ton* believed she would kill herself. The gossip was truly overwhelming. Even Fanny had admitted it might be best if she lay low for some time. Aunt Agatha's arrival a few days later had put an end to it. Georgette was sent back to the country in disgrace.

She had also been hurt by the Duke, if she was being entirely honest. He had saved her, yes, but there had been no word since she left the ball. She knew she should expect nothing more. The Duke had saved her because he was in the business of saving people. He certainly was not interested in more.

How had she fallen in love with him? How had she allowed this to happen? She had sworn she would never again lose her dignity over a man. And look what had happened: she'd found herself standing at the top of the stair, with people shrieking she wanted to throw herself off the banister because of him. Her dignity had been lost once again. It was not for him, she told herself. It was for her country, but she knew that was a lie. She had thrown caution to the winds once again, and look where it got her.

Georgette supposed she should be grateful, She still had her home in the country. If some people gave her a wide berth, most of the others were incredibly kind. And she still had her books and her music, her mathematics. The curate still exchanged cryptograms with her, and Fanny still sent her letters, deploring Aunt Agatha's behavior and Mr. Rupert Fellows' clumsy feet. She smiled thinking of her cousin.

And she had this field, with its wildflowers and butterflies. And the sun was out. She took off her bonnet and allowed the sun to hit her face. Freckles be damned.

It will get better, she thought. Someday she would not love him so much. Soon, no doubt, she would be able to go hours, or even days, without thinking of him. Without remembering those few precious moments in his company, which she had wanted to never end.

It will get better. It will.

L ADY J UDITH and Sebastien had descended upon Eversley Manor, with no warning at all and they made themselves quite at home.

"You will not believe who we saw last month, at the Drummonds' house party." Judith said.

The Duke, who was busy attempting to put his estate to rights, had been mildly annoyed by their arrival, but also accepted it as his penance.

He had neglected his family. And his friends. Although his opinion of Judith and Sebastien was no longer very great, he had done nothing to foster a relationship with them over the last ten years. He was as much to blame as they were for the coldness in their relationships. He had been so caught up in Blanche, so caught up in the dead, that he had forgotten the living.

"Miss Markham," Judith was saying. "You remember. That bouncy blonde cousin of Miss Quinby's?"

Miss Quinby. Eversley carefully set down his tea. "Oh? And how is Miss Markham?"

Sebastien chuckled. "She bade us to tell you she is bloody awful and it is entirely your fault."

"Did she? Was there any elaboration?" Eversley asked.

"Her aunt, Agatha Markham, has re-assumed chaperon duties, after Miss Quinby's scandalous behavior at the Fletcher Masquerade."

Eversley nodded. He knew this. He had been informed by her butler, when he called at Miss Quinby's townhome, that she was no longer in Town, and her aunt requested he cease any visits.

"Was it really true?" Judith asked. "Did she really threaten to kill herself over you? You were at the masquerade, were you not?"

Eversley shook his head. "No," he said. "She was not threatening to kill herself. In fact, she was doing me a rather extraordinary favor, distracting the crowd."

"Heavens, Eversley, were you doing something naughty?" Judith asked. She took out her handkerchief and waved it around her face.

He winked at her. Better to let her think that, rather than that he had been secreting two bodies in a closet.

His sister laughed. "I wouldn't have thought it possible, after Blanche."

She looked at him. "I suppose it is a good thing. You do seem much happier," she said. "You smile more. You don't hate me so very much."

He looked at her in surprise. "I never hated you, sister" he said. "What are you on about?"

Judith sniffed. "When Sebastien and I...and then Blanche...I thought you must hate me, for running away right when she died. You never visited. Hardly ever wrote. And then when I heard you'd been friendly with Miss Quinby, oh, I don't know. I know I was ugly about her, but I felt as if you were doing it to spite me."

Eversley blinked. "No, Judith. I still do not believe that what happened to Miss Quinby was right, but I never hated you. And I certainly never spoke to her out of spite. And my neglect of you and Sebastien over the past decade has been my fault alone. I was mired in my grief. I never meant you to think I wished to punish you."

Sebastien rested a hand on his wife's shoulder. "Thank you, old boy," he said. "It's good to know."

Lady Judith wiped away a tear. "Is she the reason?" she asked.

"Beg your pardon?" Eversley asked, as he raised his cup once more.

"Is Miss Quinby the reason you seem happier?"

He sighed and looked down into his tea. "I have not seen Miss Quinby since the Fletcher Masquerade," he said.

He wished he had seen her. He wanted to see her. He wanted to speak with her, to tell her about the improvements he was making, the new sheets of music he'd received from Vienna.

"You haven't?" Judith asked. "Whatever is wrong with you?"

"What? Nothing is wrong with me."

"You said she did you a favor," Judith said. "She became a complete disgrace, she can never show her face in Town again, you know."

"I, er...."

"And apparently she did this for you! As a favor to you? And you have not even seen her?" Lady Judith was beginning to sound a bit upset. Was his sister upset with him on Miss Quinby's behalf?

"I called at her townhome a few days later," he said. "She was no longer in Town."

"Ah," Sebastien said. "The dreaded Aunt Agatha had already descended to ruin Miss Markham's life."

"Fanny said you brought her music," Judith said. "She

said Miss Quinby was quite entranced with you, although she refused to admit it."

"So you spoke to Miss Markham at length, then?" he asked.

"I quite like her," Judith said. "She reminds me of me at that age. Terribly stifled and overwhelmed by attention from suitors who only wanted my money."

"That would have been me," Sebastien said.

"Yes, but then you decided you loved me after all," Judith said. "So it worked out in the end."

The two of them smiled at each other. Eversley knew that smile. It was the smile of a shared secret, the smile between two people who knew that the other one loved them, that together they would always be safe. He and Blanche had shared that smile.

Blanche. She had not come since the Fletcher Masquerade. He suspected she might stay away forever, or only stop by for momentous occasions. She had called him an idiot. 'No my idiot, you do not need me' she had said. But he did. He loved her still. He would always love her. His heart would always be hers.

But perhaps there could be a shared custody? Perhaps he could give it once more.

Oh, what was he thinking? Miss Quinby had merely been assisting him. She might have cared for him a bit, but not as much as he did her. Which was a considerable amount, if he was being entirely honest. An exceptional amount.

"Fanny wished for us to tell you something," Judith said.

He shook his head and focused on his sister. "What?" he asked.

"She wished for you to know that Miss Quinby has done the thing she swore to never do again, whatever that means. She would not explain it to me. She said you should know what it was."

Eversley slowly took a sip of tea. His heart was pounding and his palms were suddenly sweaty. He set his cup back down and wiped his wet hands on his knees.

"Thank you, Judith," he said.

"Mmmmm," Judith murmured as she eyed him up and down, no doubt taking in his sudden flush.

"Any chance she said where Miss Quinby had gone to?" he asked.

Lady Judith raised her eyebrow. "What? Are you going to run off again, and leave me and Sebastien alone to rattle around the estate by ourselves?"

"I promise to return as soon as I am able," he said. "But there is something I must do. I should have done earlier."

Judith's lips quirked. "I supposed you must see about a horse?"

"Precisely," Eversley said.

Sebastien laughed. "You dog," he said. "I wouldn't have believed it."

Judith reached down and traced the embroidery of the tablecloth. "It must be her?" she asked. "Out of all of the lovely ladies of the *Ton*, it must be her?"

Eversley swallowed and nodded. "Yes," he said. "I believe out of all of the ladies, it must be her."

She sighed. "I suppose there is a poetic sort of justice about it all," she said. She gave a small grin. "Blanche always did like her, you know. She'd be happy about it, I believe."

"You speak too soon, sister," Eversley said. "I do not even know where the lady is yet, much less her sentiments towards myself."

"She's in Somerset. Her family has a manor near a Highfield village."

The Duke stood. "Then that is where I will go."

He strode to the door of the breakfast room, and then turned back to look at his sister, who had reached for Sebastien's hand.

"I do believe you are right, Judith," he said. "Blanche would be happy about it."

"*Mais oui*," Sebastien said, his voice mimicking Blanche's.

"*Bien sur*," Judith said.

Eversley smiled.

24

*G*eorgette made her way down the lane to Highfield, the estate that had originally belonged to her parents and now belonged to her. She could not complain, she supposed. She might be a pariah, but at least she was a wealthy pariah with lovely servants and an abundance of strawberries; which she was carrying in her apron. She had already eaten her fill of them and probably had stained lips with their juices, like an urchin.

She made her way around to the side entrance and down to the kitchen, dumping the strawberries into a bowl provided by the housekeeper who promised to serve them with cream.

"I'm afraid I ate quite the number of them right from the vine," Georgette admitted.

"I'm sure," the housekeeper said. "There was a note for you, Miss. A man brought it by not an hour ago."

"A note?"

"I left it on the entrance table."

Georgette stared at the paper. It was a cryptogram.

22-19-1-23-8-'-7 20-3-26-26-13
15-8 20-3-9-6 3-'-17-26-3-17-25

How odd. The curate never left them for her here. He simply handed them off after Sunday's service. And the housekeeper would not have called him a man. He was the curate. Perhaps Fletcher had gotten loose and decided to murder her again? No. That was just her imagination running away with her.

She had read in the broadsheets about Lord Fletcher's betrayal. He had been tried for treason and hanged. It was all very sad. There had been no mention of anyone else involved. She supposed that was some relief. Enough scandal attached to her name already.

She scanned the numbers. The last word had to be "o'clock," if she was not mistaken. A time, then.

She took the note up to her secretary, and pulled out a piece of parchment and a fresh quill. It was relatively quick work, and a simple cipher.

HERMIT'S FOLLY
AT FOUR O'CLOCK

She looked at the clock on the mantel piece. Heavens! It was almost four o'clock now.

For a moment she remained still, undecided. Should she go? Who would leave her such a note? This could not be good. No, she would not go. If the man wished to see her again, he could once more visit the house. It had to be him. What if it wasn't? She was a lady alone. She was done putting herself in dangerous positions.

Right. She would not go. She had learned the lesson of impetuous decisions. There would be no going to The Hermit's Folly.

Oh, bother. Who was she trying to fool?

She ran out of the house, still wearing her strawberry stained apron. She forgot her bonnet, and her hair began to fly from her pins.

The Hermit's Folly sat atop a small hill behind the house, the product of a previous inhabitant, who had decided to build a cottage and install a hermit in it. There was no longer a hermit, but the cottage remained, a ruin now, an ode to beauty in peril. Georgette frequently walked up to take in the view from the structure.

She ran up it now.

He was standing up on the platform, looking down at her.

"I thought you might not come," Eversley said.

"I strongly considered not doing so," Georgette replied. She breathed heavily in and out; glad she was wearing a unrestrictive day dress and apron. "But then I became overwhelmed with hope."

She raised her hand to her hair. "I ran here," she said. "I must look a mess."

"I saw you running and you do not look a mess," he said. "You look lovely."

She laughed. "Liar," she said, but she smiled.

He stared down at her, and then held out her hand to help her up.

Georgette felt the tingle travel up her arm as she touched him. She could not believe he was here. Perhaps she was dreaming him.

"What are you doing here?" she asked.

"I thought I would see the sights of the area," Eversley said. "Somerset is glorious this time of year."

"Ah," she said. Her heart fell a bit. He was not here for her. What had she been thinking? He would not come here for her.

She had sworn she would never fall in love again. She had sworn she could not bear it. But looking at him, in the afternoon light, the green of Somerset stretching out behind him, she realized she may as well have said she would not breathe again. It was unavoidable. She could not have stopped it.

But this love felt different. Not the same, overwhelming love she had felt for Sebastian. Now that she was older, she could see that as the desperate infatuation of a young girl. What she felt for the man standing in front of her was stronger, and deeper, yet less tumultuous. He did not love her, but she would survive. If you truly loved someone, you could not expect them to love you back. You had to be content with knowing that you loved them, that you would give them your all, if only they asked.

Still. It would have been nice if he loved her back, she could not help thinking.

The Duke shook his head. "That is not exactly true," he said. "I did not come here to see the sights. I came here to see you."

"Oh," Georgette said. Her heart began to beat ever so slightly faster.

"Your cousin and my sister have become friends," he said.

Georgette blinked.

"Are they here?" she asked. She was confused. Was he here because of Fanny and Lady Judith?

"No, I am alone," he said. "What I meant was that Fanny told Judith to tell me to find you. Your cousin is still quite set on us making a match, you know."

Georgette nodded understanding. "I would apologize for Fanny," she said, "but you are aware of her determination. You did not need to trouble yourself. She is given to flights of fancy."

"Unlike you."

"Yes."

"You are quite the practical woman."

"Yes."

He nodded and dropped her hand, which he had still been holding, after helping her up. He strode over to the other side of the folly and looked down. He appeared agitated. What was amiss? Was it something to do with his business for the King?

He opened his mouth and closed it. Then strode to another view. Then back to Georgette, where he stood in front of her, running his hand through his hair. Georgette stood in silence, watching him, wondering what he would say.

"I do believe," he finally said, "that your cousin has a rather good point."

⌒⟋◦⟍⌒

OH LORD. What was he doing? Miss Quinby didn't want to marry him. She did not love him. She had told him, that first night that she did not ever intend to fall in love again.

Perhaps he could suggest it as a convenient arrangement. He could explain that he wished to have a companion, someone with whom he shared interests.

Yes, he could propose that way. Surely she would be amenable to such a suggestion. If for no other reason than she would be a Duchess, effectively quelling the gossips, and also have companionship.

But now the Duke was pacing in front of her, his stomach full of butterflies.

He swallowed.

"I do believe that your cousin has a rather good point," he said to her.

Silence.

He looked over to Miss Quinby. Her eyes were wide and her lips had parted. They were quite red. Was that strawberry juice? He wondered. She closed her lips and swallowed. He could see a blush creep up her cheeks.

"Oh?" She was trying to sound casual.

She was not unaffected.

Could it be? He knew what falling in love with someone felt like. He remembered it. This was different from that first heady fall he'd experienced with Blanche, but no less right. There was no way he could be experiencing this alone.

"Yes," he said. He came forward and took her hands in

his. "I believe both of us once said that we would never love again."

BOTH HAD SAID they would never love again. He was reminding her. Reminding her that he would never love anyone but Blanche. And yet he had just suggested Fanny had a good point, regarding marriage.

"We did," Georgette said, faintly. "We, neither of us wished to fall in love again. Your heart could not bear it, nor could my dignity. It was something we had in common, when you spoke to me at the ball...in the garden."

"It seems so long ago," he said. "So much has occurred."

She nodded. "I'm afraid the masquerade got a bit tricky," she said. "The guests believed I wanted to jump, and I allowed them to think so. But then I did not know how to correct the rumor in later days, and so I fled here, Your Grace,"

She was so formal. When had she started to call him Your Grace again?

"Dignity be damned," he said.

She said nothing, but her eyes widened at his frank language.

"I heard Aunt Agatha also appeared," he said.

"She did," Georgette said. "I am banned from chaperoning Fanny."

"And Miss Markham feels quite bereft, as I

understand it," he said. "She's even taken to befriending my sister."

Georgette laughed. "If anyone can befriend Lady Judith, it would be Fanny."

"I did try to call on you, a few days later," he said. "But you had already departed."

Georgette wanted to tell him that he could have written, but looking back now she wondered how she would have responded to a letter. She had felt so unmoored after the Fletcher masquerade. Her dignity, her heart, her shock at the actions of Lord Fletcher. In a way, she had needed the peace she had found in Somerset.

"You did cause quite a scandal," he said as understanding came to him. He was indeed an idiot.

"You needn't sound quite so entertained by that fact," Georgette said, somewhat grumpily.

"You lost your pride then and there," he said.

That was unnecessary, she thought. The Duke did not need to point out the lost of her pride even if it was true.

"Which is why I, for my part, would like to amend my half," he said.

"Amend?" she echoed. "Your half, of what?" What was he on about? He was speaking of her embarrassment and her destroyed reputation and now he was saying he wished to amend something? She clasped her hands and stared down at them. Her fingers were covered with strawberry juice. She looked like a common farm wench.

"Yes," he said. "If you could sacrifice your dignity once more, surely I could sacrifice my heart?"

"What exactly do you mean, Your Grace?" Georgette said. Her mind was awhirl.

"Eversley," he said. "No. Charles."

She stared at him.

"I said I would never fall in love again. Now I would like to say that I will never fall in love again, except with you," he said.

"Except with me?"

"That's right," he said. "Only with you."

"You will fall in love with me?" she asked. Her words felt slow, her mind felt fogged. He would fall in love with her?

"Have," he said. "I have fallen in love with you, Miss Quinby."

He loved her. He *loved* her. He loved *her*. Oh Good God, he loved her. He was standing in front of her and he was real and this was not a dream and he was saying that he loved her.

GEORGETTE STOOD THERE, looking dazed. Eversley could hear a bird call, the sound of cows mooing. The summer sounds of Somerset. What if she told him to go to the Devil? What if she told him she wanted nothing to do with him?

Oh God, what if she was in love with someone else?

Then she raised her face to him, smiling. "I like that amendment," she said. "I like it very much."

His heart started beating again.

"You do?" he asked.

"I do," she said. She laughed. "You see, it is past tense with me as well. I've fallen in love with you as well...Charles."

She looked so beautiful, so happy. Her hair was tangled, and she was wearing an apron smeared with what he hoped was juice or jam. She had recent freckles on her nose, and her smile was so true and genuine and real that for a moment he lost his breath.

She was real. She was real and she loved him.

He grasped her hands and pulled her towards him, and she looked up at him trust in her eyes and was that strawberries on her cheek?

"I am terribly relieved," he said. And then, with one final tug, he drew her into his arms and kissed her. She smelled of strawberries. She tasted of strawberries.

EPILOGUE

anny Markham closed the letter she had only just received and grinned. If anyone had been wandering by, they might have said that Miss Markham looked distinctly pleased with herself. She bit her lip, trying to contain her glee.

The letter, posted from Somerset, contained the very happy information that Miss Georgette Quinby, more recently known to the *Ton* as The Mad Heiress, had accepted an offer of marriage from the Duke of Eversley.

"And they shall love one another for the rest of their lives," Fanny said out loud.

And she was right. She only hoped that she could be so lucky in love.

CONTINUE READING FOR A SNEAK PEEK OF...

The Duke's Daughter ~ Lady Amelia Atherton
by Isabella Thorne

1

_____

With a few lines of black ink scrawled on cream parchment, her life had changed forever. Lady Amelia had to say goodbye, but she could not bear to. She sat alone in the music room contemplating her future. Outside the others gathered, but here it was quiet. The room was empty apart from the piano, a lacquered ash cabinet she had received as a gift from her father on her twelfth birthday. She touched a key and the middle C echoed like the voice of a dear friend. The bench beneath her was the same one she had used when she begun learning, some ten years ago, and was as familiar to her as her father's armchair was to him.

Lighter patches on the wood floor marked where the room's other furniture had sat for years, perhaps for as long as she had been alive. New furnishings would arrive, sit in different places, make new marks, but she would not be here to see it. Amelia ran her fingers across the keys, not firmly enough to make a sound, but she heard the notes in her head regardless. When all her world was turmoil, music had been a constant comforting presence. Turmoil. Upheaval. Chaos. What was the proper word for her life now?

She breathed in a calming breath, and smoothed her dark skirt, settling it into order. She would survive; she would smile again, but first, she thought, she would play. She would lose herself in the music, this one last time.

TWO WEEKS EARLIER

LADY AMELIA LOOKED the gentleman over. Wealthy, yes, but not enough to make up for his horrid appearance. *That* would take considerably more than mere wealth. He leered at her as though she were a pudding he would like to sample. Though it was obvious he was approaching to ask her to dance, she turned on her heel in an unmistakable gesture and pretended to be in deep conversation with her friends. Refusing the man a dance outright would be gauche, but if her aversion was apparent enough before the man ever asked, it would save them both an embarrassment. She smoothed her rich crimson gown attempting to project disinterest. It was a truly beautiful garment; silk brocade with a lush velvet bodice ornamented with gold and pearl accents.

Lady Charity, one of Amelia's friends in London, smiled, revealing overly large teeth. The expression exaggerated the flaw, but Charity had other attributes.

"That is an earl you just snubbed," said Charity, wide-eyed. It both galled and delighted Lady Charity the way Amelia dismissed gentlemen. Lady Amelia did not approve of the latter, she did not take joy in causing others discomfort. It was a necessity, not a sport.

"Is he still standing there looking surprised?" Amelia asked, twirling one of her golden ringlets back into place with the tip of a slender gloved finger. Looking over her shoulder to see for herself would only confuse the man into thinking she was playing coy. "I am the daughter of a duke, Charity. I need not throw myself at every earl that comes along."

"Thank goodness, or you would have no time for anything else." Charity's comment bore more than a tinge of jealousy.

Lady Amelia's debut earlier this Season had drawn the attention of numerous suitors, and the cards still arrived at her London townhouse in droves. Each time she went out, whether to a ball or to the Park, she was inundated with tireless gentlemen. If she were a less patient woman, it would have become tedious. Gracious as she was, Amelia managed to turn them all down with poise. Lady Amelia's father, the Duke of Ely, was a kind man who doted on his only daughter but paid as little mind to her suitors as Amelia herself; always saying there was plenty of time for such things. Her debut like most aspects of her upbringing was left to the professionals. What do I pay tutors for? He had said, when a younger Amelia had asked him a question on the French verbs. There had been many tutors. Amelia had learned the languages, the arts, the histories, music and needlepoint until she was, by Society's standards, everything a young woman should be. She glanced across the hall to that same father, and found him deep in conversation with several white haired men, no doubt some of the older lords talking politics as they were wont to do. She flashed him a quick smile and he toasted her with his glass.

Father had even indulged her by hiring a composer to teach her the piano, after she proven herself adept and eager to learn. If any of these flapping popinjays were half the man her father was...she thought with irritation.

Lady Patience, the less forward of Lady Amelia's friends, piped in, "Men are drawn to your beauty like moths to a flame." Her voice had a sad quality to it.

"I'm sure you will find the perfect beau, Patience." Amelia replied.

"Yes, well, you might at least toss them our way, when you have decided against them." Charity said. She peeked wide eyed over her slivered fan which covered her bosom with tantalizing art. Amelia's eyes were brought back to her friends and she smiled.

While Charity was blonde and buxom, Patience was diminutive, yet cursed with garish red hair. The wiry, unruly locks had the habit of escaping whatever style her maid attempted, leaving the girl looking a bit like a waif, frazzled and misplaced at an elegant ball like the one they were attending. Though her dress was a lovely celestial blue frock trimmed round the bottom with lace and a white gossamer polonaise long robe joined at the front with rows of satin beading.

Charity's flaws were more obvious, apart from her wide mouth. She had a jarring laugh, and wore necklines so low they barely contained her ample bosom. The gown she was wearing extenuated this feature with many row of white scalloped lace and a rosy pink bodice clasped just underneath. It bordered on vulgar. Amelia intended to make the polite suggestion on their next shopping trip that Lady Charity perhaps should purchase an extra yard of fabric so she might have enough for an *entire* dress.

"Do not be foolish, Patience. You deserve someone wonderful. If we must be married, it should be to someone that... excites us," Amelia said, rising up onto her toes and clasping her hands in front of her breast.

Her comment caused Patience to flush with embarrassment. It was easy to forget Patience was two years older than Amelia and a year older than Charity, for her naivety gave her a childlike demeanor.

"Not all of us are beautiful enough to hold out for someone handsome," said Patience. When she blushed, her freckles blended with the rosiness of her cheeks. Her eyes alighted with hope, and she was pretty in a shy sort of way.

Charity nodded her agreement, but Amelia frowned and clasped Patience's hands. "You are sweet and bright and caring. Any man would be lucky to have you for his wife. Do not settle because you feel you have no choice. The right man will come along. Just you wait and see."

Tears swelled in Patience's bright blue eyes. Amelia hoped she would not begin to cry; the girl was prone to hysterics and leaps of emotion. Charity was only a notch better, and if one girl began the other was certain to follow. Two crying girls was not the spectacle Amelia hoped to make at a ball. She clapped her hands together and twirled around, so her skirts fanned out around her feet.

"Come now; let us find some of those handsome men to dance with. It should not be hard for three young ladies like us." Amelia glanced back.

Patience was wiping at her eyes and fidgeting with her dress— no matter how many times Amelia scolded her for it, the girl could not quit the nervous and irritating gesture—which generally wrinkled her dress with two fist sized wads on either side of her waist. Meanwhile Charity was puffing out her chest like a seabird. One more deep breath and she was sure to burst her seams.

It would be up to Amelia, then. In a matter of minutes she had snagged two gentlemen and placed one with Charity and one with Patience on the promise that she herself would dance with them afterward. Though men waited around her, looking hopefully in her direction, none dared approach until she gave them a sign of interest. She had already earned a reputation of being discerning with whom she favored, and no man wanted the stigma of having been turned away. Amelia perused the ballroom at her leisure, silently wishing for something more than doters and flatterers after her father's influence.

SAMUEL BERESFORD DID NOT WANT to be here. He found balls a tremendous waste of time, the dancing and the flirting and, thinly veiled beneath it all, the bargaining.

For that was what marriage boiled down to, a bargain. It was all about striking a deal where each person involved believed they had the advantage over the other. If it were not for his brother's pleading, he would never been seen at a fancy affair like this. Dressed in his naval uniform, a blue coat with gold epaulets and trimmings and white waistcoat and breeches, he attracted more attention than he wished.

"Stop scowling, Samuel," said Percival as he returned to his brother's side from a brief sojourn with a group of lords. "You look positively dour."

"Did you find the man?" Samuel inquired.

Percival sipped his wine and shook his head. "It is no matter. Let us concentrate on the women. We should be enjoying their company and you seem intent on scaring them all off with your sour expression."

Unlike himself, Samuel's older brother Percival loved the frivolity of these occasions. As the eldest son of an earl it was very nearly an obligation of his office to enjoy them, so Samuel could not begrudge his brother doing his duty.

"You think it my expression and not our looks that are to blame?" Samuel asked, only half in jest. To appease his brother he hid his scowl behind the rim of his wine glass.

The Beresford brothers were not of disagreeable appearance, but they lacked the boyish looks so favored at the moment. They did not look gentlemanly, the brothers were too large, their features too distinctly masculine, for the women to fawn and coo over. Additionally Samuel had been sent to the Royal Naval Academy at the age of twelve, a life that had led him to be solidly built, broad across the chest and shoulders. He felt a giant amongst the gentry.

"Smile a bit brother, and let us find out." Percy elbowed Samuel in the side.

─·──◦◦◦◦──·─

CONTINUE READING....

The Duke's Daughter ~ Lady Amelia Atherton

or

Buy
The Ladies of Bath
3 Full Length Novel Collection

WANT EVEN MORE REGENCY ROMANCE...

Follow Isabella Thorne on BookBub
https://www.bookbub.com/profile/isabella-thorne

Sign up for my VIP Reader List!
at
https://isabellathorne.com/

Receive weekly updates from Isabella and an
EXCLUSIVE FREE STORY

Like Isabella Thorne on Facebook
https://www.facebook.com/isabellathorneauthor/

Made in the USA
Monee, IL
16 November 2020